Axis Stone Mysteries

GOD'S DOOR

G. L. Keady

TABLE OF CONTENTS

CHAPTER
ONE

'B urnt out' was the diagnosis from my doctor; a prescription for a break away from cell phones was his prognosis. He handed me a prescription for something akin to Prozac, called Zoloft, which sounded like the name of a German footballer, and then sent me on my way. Leaving the surgery lighter in the pocket and catching the desperate expressions on the faces of waiting patients, I shot a wink at the cute receptionist. But upon self-diagnosing that I wasn't suffering from depression, I crumpled up the prescription and filed it in the cylindrical floor filing system under 'not that desperate.'

A brisk walk, bundled up to shield myself from the cold, cursing global warming for freezing me, brought me to the Regis Office building. As I brushed the snow off my overcoat at the door, Linus hobbled up behind me.

"You did well, son."

"How's that, Linus?"

"Your ma and pa would be proud of you," he said, patting me on the back like he was trying to make me burp.

"Yeah, well, it took a team—we all played a role. How's Booker?"

"Down with a cold; this weather gets right into your bones."

"It does. It was quite amusing to see how quickly my LAPD friend Santana high-tailed it back to L.A once we'd wrapped up the case."

"They can't handle the cold on the west coast. One day's the same as the other over there ... at least we've got seasons."

I decided to take the staircase instead of the elevator; that's about as close as I've been able to get to exercise since I arrived in the Big Apple. Kendy was at her desk, her eyes glued to her laptop screen when I arrived, puffing. She looked up as if I had startled her.

"It's just me."

"I heard heavy footsteps, like running, and thought we were like about to get busted or something."

"Nope, just me trying to get a bit of cardiovascular activity to warm me up, it's bloody freezing outside."

"Ah, you'll get used to it," she said matter-of-factly, as if it's just to be expected. She got up and poured me a coffee. "Here, this'll warm you up."

I flopped into my chair and took the mug with both hands, enjoying its heat thawing out my frozen fingers. Kendy pulled up a chair.

"Remember Richard Harris, the guy who left a message on your nearly dead answer machine about some artefact he found that someone had since stolen?"

"Yeah, it's on the bucket list ... so?"

"Well, there was another message this morning, this time from Major Roland Harris, the guy's father. He said Richard himself has gone missing now ... sounded pretty upset."

"Did he mention the location?"

"Yeah, it's the resort Hotel Lindos in San Pedro ... I Googled it, it's in Belize in the Yucatan."

"Central America?"

"Yeah, sounds like a pretty cool place."

I reclined in my chair with the thought of a tropical holiday swimming in my mind, but the name Belize had triggered a reminder to catch up with Bella. Then the idea struck me; I could check out this exotic case and, on the way back, drop into L.A. and see Bella and Samantha.

"You there, boss? You look like you're wigging out or something."

"Sorry Kendy, I was just mulling things over. Yucatan sounds like just the place for me to chill. You take a week off with pay, call Major Harris, tell him I'll be there, and then make all the relevant bookings for me to leave ... um, tonight."

"Tonight?" She said shocked.

"Yep, when you decide on something, Kendy, act on it. That's my personal dictum."

Happy to have a paid break, she jumped up and got on with it.

"Oh, you'll need to drop by the office a couple of times through the week to check the antique answer machine and the mail, okay?"

"Can I buy a new one? You know, like a modern one?"

I thought about it; I loved my 80s Sony answer machine, but hey, I guess I should move with the times.

"Okay, but just an answer machine ... not like a cellphone with all sorts of useless complicated waggle—just keep it simple. Huh?"

She chuckled the way you do to a senior, "No worries, boss."

~ ~ ~

Like an artist's canvas, the land extended as lush and green as the cloth on a billiard table. One edge bordered by the pristine blue waters of the Caribbean Sea, dotted with palm trees, and on the other side of the dirt road, thick jungle. The panoramic vista out of the window was well worth the bumpy ride in the excuse for a bus. It had been a nine-hour flight with Aero México from NYC to Campeche International Airport. Then an hour and a half commuter flight to San Pedro. By then, I was like the walking dead when I boarded the dilapidated bus for the final leg of my pilgrimage to Hotel Lindos, situated right at the very tip of the San Pedro peninsula.

The lone passenger on board, and listening to the 'Tears for Fears' 80s hit playing on the driver's radio, the thought struck me: so everybody wants to change the world, you guys weren't wrong back then... Not a bad thing, I suppose ... but these days, in my book, change has to begin with awareness. Too often, change has been driven by greed. Plundering our natural resources, the forests, minerals—scars left as a reminder … an ugly price to pay… I looked out the window. Why the hell would you want to spoil a beautiful place like this? Just look at it … God's own country. I lowered my brown cowboy hat over my face and drifted off.

It felt like only seconds later when the loud hiss of airbrakes signalled that we were coming to a stop. I raised my hat and sat up to take in the view. I had been out for two hours, and I guess I needed the rest. If I thought what I had seen earlier was magical, then this place we were arriving at was truly awe-inspiring; it epitomised the definition of a tropical paradise. An antiquated two-storey wooden hotel from the 1930s stood before us, with an aged timber wharf extending like a weathered finger into the pristine blue waters of the Caribbean. This was the kind of place that resonated with me, a destination that exuded an old-world charm and bucolic beauty.

The bus came to a stop under the awning at the entrance of the hotel. I pulled on my trusty cowboy boots, picked up my navy-blue duffle bag, and made my way to the front of the bus. With a salute to the driver, I stepped out into the suffocating humidity that hit me like an iron fist, stealing my breath away. As the bus pulled away and executed a U-turn to head back to San Pedro, it almost vanished into the distance, its form wavering in the mirage-like shimmer of the heat. Covered in a cloud of dust stirred up from the road, I turned and headed towards the reception area.

Upon closer inspection, the hotel exuded more charm than sheer beauty, showing signs of needing a fresh coat of paint. For those who appreciated 1950s black-and-white Hollywood classics like myself, this place possessed all the classic attributes. It felt as if Humphrey Bogart and Lauren Bacall might step out through the front doors at any moment. Swinging my kit bag over my shoulder, I casually strolled inside.

The interior harmonised with the exterior, a testament to a bygone era. A few large framed oil paintings graced the timber walls, a staircase gracefully led to the second floor, and a polished timber front counter with a bell displayed a sign that read 'ring for service.'

I gave the bell a friendly tap.

Removing my hat, I revealed hair damp with perspiration, adhered to my forehead. A lovely Mayan girl in her late teens, dressed in a charming black and white maid's uniform, peeked out from a doorway. "Hello, Miss, I'd like to check..." My sentence trailed off as she vanished. In her place, a young man in his early twenties, also uniformed, appeared behind the front desk.

"Welcome to Hotel Lindos," he announced, flaunting a local native accent. "You must be Mr Axis."

He slid the register toward me for completion and handed me a ballpoint pen. There was no computer in sight, just the old-fashioned manual approach.

"What's your name?" I inquired while jotting down the necessary information.

"Boy, sir. I'm the day manager. How was your trip, Mr Axis?"

"Interesting, Boy," I replied as I returned the pen. "Just call me Axis."

"Major Harris would like to see you in the bar after you've settled into your room." He produced a key from under the desk. "I'll show you to—"

I accepted the key to Room 111. "Don't worry, Boy, I've only got a kit bag. I'll find the room. Please let the major know I'll be down in ten minutes."

Heading up the staircase, I overheard Boy calling out, "Cora, Mr Axis has checked in now. You can come out from hiding."

I couldn't help but chuckle; it was quite endearing. It also indicated that the hotel likely didn't have many guests these days.

As I unpacked a few items that required hanging, there was a knock at the door. Upon opening it, I found Cora standing there, holding fresh linens. However, it was a bit like pulling teeth to get them from her; she appeared extremely nervous.

Then, interrupting the calm atmosphere, a shrill woman's voice pierced the air as she engaged in an argument with someone in the corridor.

"You can take your holiday and shove it will never find the light of day!" the woman yelled, her voice brimming with anger. The door slammed shut so forcefully that it felt like the entire hotel shuddered. I leaned past Cora in the doorway, catching a glimpse of the corridor, but there was nothing to see. I turned back to Cora. "Unhappy guest?"

Cora simply shook her head and replied timidly, "Too much drinking, sir."

As I entered the bar, the walls greeted me with old black and white photos depicting fishing expeditions. Among the shots, I spotted a few familiar faces. At one end of the bar sat a Spanish-looking woman in her late forties, though she tried to present herself as younger. Her attire leaned more towards that of a streetwalker than a resort guest, and her excessive makeup and evident hangover gave away her bad mood. Beneath the alcohol-fuelled facade, I could sense that she had been quite attractive once upon a time.

She banged her fist on the bar, demanding attention. "Boy! Boy! Damn it!! I need a drink. Why isn't there ever any music playing in this dump?"

Boy, standing behind the bar, appeared concerned. "I'm terribly sorry, Miss Rita, but Mr Vitale has instructed that you can't have any drinks until after dark." He braced himself for the expected torrent of anger.

"I don't give a damn what Mr Vitale said! The bar is open, isn't it? I'm a customer, that means you serve me."

"So sorry, Miss Rita, but—"

She became confrontational, "What have I gotta do to get what I want around here, take my clothes off...?"

I sat quietly, trying to ignore her antics ... but at the same time enjoying her banter.

A big older man hobbled in, and it seemed to me that arthritis had taken a toll on him, causing him to walk with the assistance of two walking sticks. I estimated him to be in his late seventies, but his eyes were still as sharp as a razor.

He settled into a comfortable lounge chair.

"Oh, I wouldn't go that far, my dear Miss Gee ... It might raise a few too many eyebrows ... You could get yourself injured in the rush..." he jested.

Rita swivelled on her bar stool to face him, her mood shifting to flirtatiousness.

"I'd hope to raise more than that, my dear Mr Harris."

He smiled wryly, "Give the lady a drink, please, Boy."

"But, Mr Vitale, sir?"

"I own this establishment, Boy, not Mr Vitale," he said calmly, instructively. "So do as I say, please, and give the lady her heart starter."

Boy nodded in agreement and poured a straight scotch for the lady. She raised her glass to the old man.

"A toast to a genuine gentleman."

"Yes, dear lady, that I am. But endeavouring to stay one these days often invites more trouble than it's worth."

Rita's brow furrowed, not quite grasping his meaning. "I assume you mean you're too old to—"

He interrupted her. "I have always considered it presumptuous to assume anything about another person, Miss Gee."

I stood up from my place in the corner and approached the old man. Rita noticed me for the first time and asked, "Hmm, things are looking up. Can I buy you a drink, stranger?"

"No thanks, too early." I sat down opposite Mr Harris.

"Mr Stone, I presume?" Harris asked.

"Indeed, sir, Axis Stone," I replied, taking his hand to shake.

"Good to meet you, young fella. Glad you made it; most visitors die on the bus."

I immediately took a liking to his wit.

He struggled to stand, took his two sticks, and said, "Come to my office for a chat."

A massive man with a physique reminiscent of Mr Universe suddenly filled the doorway, casting a shadow that blocked all light, and stared at Rita until she submitted. She got up from the bar and went to him like an obedient dog. Harris, on the other hand, was prevented from passing by the imposing figure.

"You're blocking the doorway, Tong," Harris said emphatically.

The man with the large acne-scarred face, of Chinese descent, wearing a cold demeanour and an icy stare, fixed his gaze on me as I backed up Harris. Without uttering a word, Tong moved slowly, in a sloth-like motion, to stand aside and allow us to pass.

CHAPTER TWO

The study was a veritable museum of maritime memorabilia, with maps and photographs adorning the walls. The room showcased all the mandatory nautical items: a ship in a bottle, pirate paraphernalia, a cutlass, a Spanish helmet, and various bits and pieces of ship's gear. Harris obviously cherished these treasures, which might be considered junk by someone else. One particularly eye-catching item was a life-sized dummy dressed in an Irish kilt, seated in a chair by the door.

"Oh, don't mind Paddy," Harris said, settling himself into his big black leather office chair behind his antique mahogany desk. "He's just an old friend who reminds me of my Irish heritage."

"Hi, Paddy," I said, joining in on the joke.

"He won't answer you; he's just a dummy. Are you Irish as well?"

Not missing the cynical dig, I took a seat opposite Harris, a bit uneasy with Paddy's gaze on me from behind.

I noticed a framed photo on Harris's desk of a much younger version of him, minus the walking sticks, with a young man standing proudly on either side of a hung massive black marlin.

"That's quite a marlin. Who's in the photo with you?"

"My son Richard. He was one hell of a fisherman, and that was a great catch that day. He had a sixth sense for the big ones, knew exactly where they'd be. That's a real talent, you know? Great catch that day ... Hmm, did I already say that? You'll have to forgive me;

sometimes I repeat myself ... Hmm, sometimes I repeat myself. Are you a fisherman, son?"

I chuckled. "A bit, and yes, it's a talent, a real special one. It's like knowing if someone's telling you the truth or not ... that's another talent."

"Tell me, do you think a fly loops the loop?" Harris motioned with his hand. "Or does it flip over in a roll to land upside down on the ceiling?"

It was an interesting conundrum. I followed the motion with my hand and then shook my head. "You know, I can't say that I've ever noticed. But if I were to hazard a guess, I'd say it flips."

"It clearly demonstrates the observation skills of humans or lack thereof. Countless flies are doing it all the time, and we don't even notice."

"Speaking of flies ... they make me think of crap, and crap makes me think of that guy Tong out there. Is he always that friendly?"

"Young man, I don't know you from a bar of soap, but I've been trusting my instincts for almost eighty years now, and they've managed to serve me reasonably well. So, I figure I can trust you. But sure as there is day, I don't trust Tong or his boss, Vitale. If you ask me, I reckon they're a pair of scoundrels. Vitale treats that poor lass Rita like she was nothing short of compost. But that's another yarn. You obviously got my message."

"Yes, and the original message from Richard, saying someone had stolen an artefact from him."

"No, that was actually me posing as Richard, just testing the waters ... You see, I heard about you through a friend of an old friend."

"Who's that?"

"Well, I know Jeremy Yates through Colonel Witten, who knew your folks. The Colonel I go back to the Korean War ... don't suppose you heard about that one? Anyhow, I had asked Jeremy for him to recommend a private investigator, and he immediately gave me your name. My son disappeared ten years ago. Angel can tell you more about it than me."

"Angel?"

"Richard's wife. My daughter-in-law. Don't know what I'd do without her."

"Where is she? Is she here?"

"Of course, son ... she runs the place ... out right now on a fishing charter. It's a tragedy he died so young ... cut down in his prime. He had so much to live for." Harris looked out of the window, tearful.

It looked like he was either looking for his son or for the boat returning with his daughter-in-law.

"They'd only been married a week when he vanished."

"When will she be back?"

He turned from the window and wiped the tears from his old grey eyes. "By sundown. But you'll have to be gentle with her ... she's very special. Gifted, you might say ... clairvoyant ... she can read minds." He glared at me through his white bushy eyebrows, expecting a reaction, but got none.

"Does she know you've made contact with me?"

"Hell no!" he rumbled.

"Okay, then maybe if you introduced me, it would help break the ice."

"Nope, include me out. You just get yourself down to the wharf at sunset, and you'll find her there. She'll be working on the Lindos Lady by then; that's her first love."

"You talk about her like a proud father."

"That's because I am. Now, skedaddle; you look like you could do with forty winks before she gets in."

I got up. "You're not wrong."

"You know, deep down inside, I think Angel replaced my Richard ... took over his job, his skills ... even some of his mannerisms ... A real tomboy, could work the tattoos of any sailor. Yep, sometimes it's like having my boy still here with me."

A bus pulled into the forecourt, blocking the view from the bay windows.

"Must be midday already. Last bus for the day ... How time flies," Roland observed.

I made for the door and stopped, "Yep, sometimes it loops the loop; other times, it just rolls by."

Roland chuckled, "Well done, lad. See, my ceiling theory becomes relevant. You know we're expecting a famous actor on that bus."

"Thanks for your time, Mr Harris."

"Call me Roland. I'm only sorry I couldn't be of more help. In the meantime, the place is yours. Oh, if you want to take a look at Richard's journal," he pulled open the desk drawer, produced a leather-bound book, and handed it to me. "I'm sure Angel won't mind."

I took the journal and, on the way out the door, patted Paddy on the head. "Catch you later, Paddy."

I heard Roland mumble to himself, "Won't answer you, son, Paddy's a dummy. Thought I told him that ... strange fellow, must be Irish."

Made me smile.

As I walked past reception on my way upstairs, I noticed a burly Chinese man in a white suit and wearing a white safari hat checking in with a bespectacled Chinese woman who gave the impression she was his PA. Cora was behind the door taking a shy peek at the actor, like playing a kid's game. I didn't recognise the Chinaman at all.

"The room must have a king-sized bed, my friend ... and, not rock hard. We plan on spending a lot of time in it. Don't we, baby?" he bellowed a little louder than he needed to.

"No problem, Mr Chan," Boy replied nervously. "Here's your key, Sir; you'll be in 112. I'll bring your bags."

As I was going up the staircase, I looked down; they had more bags than a Japanese tour group. I figured it would take Boy the rest of the day to lug them up to the room.

As I reached the landing at the top of the stairs, I heard the woman say in a small voice but still audible in the cavernous lobby,

"Carmen wants to go for a swim in the ocean. Carmen is hot."

I thought that's odd, why is she talking in the first person?

After a shower, a shave, and a change of clothes, I chose not to rest and decided to take a walk. As I came out of my room with the diary under my arm, I found Mr Chan and Carmen coming out of their room across the hall, changed into beachwear and carrying towels. Chan lowered his sunglasses and peered over them at me.

I said to Chan conversationally, "Hi there, certainly warm enough to hit the beach."

I noticed when he smiled in a friendly manner, he had a gold front tooth, and that instantly reminded me of my Filipino mercenary friend Dan.

"The name's Chan, Charlie Chan, and my girlfriend here is Carmen. You're?"

"Axis Stone, pleased to meet you both."

Carmen almost disappeared behind the hulk of Chan. I couldn't help but notice how muscular his legs were in shorts.

"Heading down?" he asked.

"Just got here today as well, on the earlier bus. Thought I'd go for a walk and take it all in."

We walked together toward the staircase. "One hell of a trip getting here," he confided.

"You're not kidding, the last leg was a doozy. I swear I nearly lost my teeth with that bumpy ride. I'm told you're a Hollywood actor?"

"Yes, well, that's a work in progress. Charlie Chan was a fictional Honolulu police detective created by the author Earl Derr Biggers for a series of mystery novels. It was loosely based on a real Hawaiian PI named Chang Apana, my grandfather on my mother's side. Oddly enough, my mother married a Chan, and they chose to name me after the Hollywood character ... which didn't fare so well for me when I began attending auditions."

We both dropped our keys in the box on the reception desk and proceeded outside.

"That's a bit of a coincidence; my parents were a famous crime fiction writing team."

We stopped on the forecourt.

"And they were?"

"The Carter Stone mystery series."

"Of course, very famous indeed. So you've followed in their exceedingly large footsteps then?"

"No, I just live in their shadow."

"Oh, don't be too ticklish about that Mr Stone, my grandfather used to say; if a man is too ticklish … he might not hear what is said to him beyond his own laughter."

"Thank you for that little anecdote Mr Chan. Might catch you at happy hour. Nice meeting you both."

They made their way on the footpath toward the beach while I walked toward the wharf, where I could see a large modern game fishing vessel moored at its end, a little out of character compared to the vintage hotel and wharf. I liked Chan but thought it best to keep my profession to myself for the time being.

With the sea breeze cooling me down, I traversed the hundred metres of the wharf to the workshop at the end. I looked down at the Lindos Lady tethered to bollards on the wharf. It wasn't rocking about as the sea was calm, but still, it heightened my distaste for anything nautical. A person appeared from out of a hatch, dressed in coveralls and a sailor's cap.

"G'day mate," I greeted the person. When the grease-smeared face peered up at me, I could tell it was a woman. "Oh, I'm sorry, Mrs Harris, I thought—"

"I'm not a mate; I'm the captain. What can I do for you?"

I offered my hand down to shake. When she took it, I immediately experienced a short flash of insight in my mind, accompanied by a voice, her voice that said, "You're blocking me, why?"

I let go of her hand as though it had given me an electric shock. She'd left a wad of grease on my palm and giggled in a cute boyish fashion, "Sorry, I guess I greased your palm."

It was obvious she shared Roland's sense of eccentric humour.

"Axis Stone," I said, remembering Roland had mentioned she was clairvoyant, and that might explain the inner voice and flash.

"Angel Harris."

She suddenly noticed the diary under my arm, and her expression soured. "That's my husband's journal ... what are you doing with it?"

"Oh, yes, I hope you don't mind."

"Did I have a choice?" she said in an obvious huff.

She turned abruptly to continue her work.

"I've never experienced that before."

With her back to me, she asked, "What's that?"

"Your voice in my head saying you're blocking me."

She looked up and shading her eyes with her hand said, "It might have been because I was blocking you."

"Well, it could be a good start if we stopped blocking each other."

"A start to what, Mr Stone?"

I could feel her stare probing my mind.

"You're cheating," I said.

"Sorry, but I need to know if you're of the light or dark side. You can read the journal, but only if you promise to leave me alone."

"Deal ... but only if you have dinner with me tonight."

"That's hardly leaving me alone, Mr Stone. No, I'm sorry ... house rules ... no fraternising with the—"

"Enemy?"

"Guests, Mr Stone, the guests."

"I won't take no for an answer, but you already know that, don't you? See you at seven."

Deep in thought, she watched me make my way back along the pier toward the hotel. I was sensing that I could well remind her of Richard somehow.

Mission accomplished, I was about to enter the hotel lobby when I noticed Rita sitting alone on the porch. She had changed her clothes and hairstyle to look less provocative and more Spanish. She looked in my direction, took a long drag on her cigarette, and blew a stream of smoke into the air. I approached her like a bullfighter entering the ring. Her pose was picture postcard perfect, framed like a Pablo Picasso painting. I stopped and playfully stamped my foot Flamenco style. A big smile broke on her face. I turned sharply, stamped again, and as I went through the entrance doors, I heard her call out after me, "Bravo! Mucho, macho!"

I had just set foot in the lobby and was greeted by a savage punch in the solar plexus. The journal tumbled onto the floor, and the word 'Macho' echoed in my mind as I dropped to one knee gasping for air, winded. Through the haze, I heard Boy's voice objecting, "No! Senor! No!"

I peered up at Tong, standing over me like a colossus. Then a scream came from Rita. "What do you think you're doing, Tong!"

She dropped to her knees to assist me, but before she could, the silent statue Tong grasped her by the arm and literally dragged her to her feet, then through the doors outside with her protesting all the way.

"Let go of me, you ape. You're hurting my arm!"

Boy rushed over to help me up.

CHAPTER
THREE

I had just sat down at a table in the dining room when Angel arrived. She was dressed casual. I stood and pulled out a chair for her. Just then Charlie, dressed in a dinner suit, and Carmen in a body-hugging ankle-length Chanel black dress, took a table near ours. As Charlie pulled out the chair for Carmen, he cracked, "Good evening, extras."

"Extras?" I complained, "I had no idea we'd been cast in your little play, Chan. A dose of narcissism perhaps?"

"Goes with the suit, Mr Stone ... Life is but a stage on which we're all players ... Some of us are stars," he nodded at Angel, then turned his attention to me, "and some of us are extras."

"If everyone is in your play, sir, then it's no longer a play; it is an audience," Angel responded.

"That depends entirely upon your perspective, Mrs Harris."

After the verbal jousting, Charlie sat opposite Carmen.

"How did he know who I am?" Angel asked me.

A trio was on the small dance floor and broke into a low-key bossa nova instrumental of "Fool on the Hill." I used my knowledge of the lyrics as a conversational metaphor.

"I guess you can feel like you're sitting alone on a hill sometimes ... but it's what you choose, isn't it?"

Angel also knew the lyrics. "Ah, the man with the perfect grin ... Let's get one thing perfectly clear. I'm not interested in talking about

Richard's disappearance, and I'm not going to have sex with you. So you can drop the foreplay and all the other deep and meaningless claptrap, okay?"

I jumped to my feet and, posing as a British public school boy, said, "Right. Shall that be all, Mum? Not a sporting start to the evening, is it? Shall we begin again then?" I shot her a comical smile. "Good evening, Mrs Harris, might I join you?"

Her stony face cracked with amusement, and peering at me through one eye, she said, "Maybe."

I resumed my seat. "Ah, now that's better. No, and no, I won't question you about your husband's disappearance, and yes, no sex, though I warn you I do practice safe sex and wear a condom at all times."

She rolled her eyes but then a certain look betrayed her fondness for me. Cora arrived with the menu. Angel didn't need to look at it.

"I'll take the fish of the day, Cora. I recommend it, Mr Stone, I caught and gutted them myself."

"Lovely … Yes, sounds fine. Same, thanks, Cora, plus a few gallons of red wine to wash it down."

Cora left, and I said, studying Angel's piercing azure blue eyes, "So, tell me about this second sight of yours?"

"Why are you and our Chinese guest over there at loggerheads?"

"Hmm, not going to answer me, hey? more verbal jousting … Then it's time to change the subject until it suits me. I guess we're continually getting off on the wrong foot. So, it's time for—" I jumped up. "Super sleuth! Able to leap tall egos in a single bound, more powerful than an egg-induced fart, and who disguised as Bill Gates fights a never-ending battle against truth, justice, in the capitalist way...."

Charlie turned towards us and said, "Hear! Hear! Very good."

Angel blushed. "Very funny. Now sit down, you're embarrassing me. You know newly arrived guests carry aggression from the city with them for a few days … then it wears off."

I sat, "Not only pretty but wise, totally full of surprises."

The conversation was suddenly suspended by the arrival of Rita on the arm of whom I suspected was Vitale, backed up by Tong. Vitale was a small, overweight, evil-looking man that oozed bad vibes. He reminded me of a gangster I had previous dealings with, Al Head.

Dressed in a cream linen suit, with a black silk shirt and copious bling, he looked every bit a gangster. He leered at everyone in the room, then selected a table for three. Once seated, his gruff voice blared rudely. "Cora! Bring me some freakin' wine."

I heard Carmen ask Charlie, "Who is that warthog?"

"Vinny Vitale, the big guy is Tong, his henchman, and his handbag is ex-lounge singer Rita Gee," said Charlie.

Vitale yelled out louder for Cora to hear from the kitchen. "Cora! Sleepy locals! Where the fuck is she?"

Intolerant of Vitale's abhorrent attitude, I could see Angel was just about to get up and give him a piece of her mind, when Cora saved the day by arriving with his bottle of wine.

Boy showed four pretty young girls to a table.

"That man is an asshole. I'm sorry, but he really gets on my goat," Angel admitted.

"You're not Robinson Crusoe ... So, how's the diving this time of year?" I asked.

"A quick change of subject ... Well, not bad but far from perfect. Since developers were allowed to strip a lot of the forest, run-off from soil erosion has clouded the water. Ultimately, the silt residue will suffocate the reef. They won't be content until they've completely destroyed it. Man's greed is responsible for far too much destruction."

"Tell me about it, everybody wants to rule the world."

Again, Vitale went off on a tirade, "This place is driving me freakin insane! The service is crap. The menu is the same shit every night. Cora!"

Angel couldn't take any more. She was just about to stand up when this time Charlie beat her to it, made his way over to Vitale and spoke to him with a put-on over-exaggerated Chinese accent. "I beg your pardon, sir, but you seem either to lack any consideration for other guests or you have little or no control over your vocal range. My Grandfather once told me ... a man with a bull's roar attracts only a lot more bull."

I could almost see the steam coming out of Vitale's ears. "Who is this fucken Asian idiot?"

"My name is Charlie Chan, and I suggest you watch your mouth in front of the ladies present."

Vitale eyeballed him, "Charlie Chan? ... You're having me on."

I got up and went over to Carmen, who was looking concerned. Tong spoke to Chan in Cantonese.

"What did he say?" I quietly asked Carmen to interpret.

"He asked 'why you insulted my friend.'"

Chan glared at Tong with a fierce look in his eyes that I certainly hadn't seen before and responded gruffly.

Carmen explained, "Charlie said your friend is acting like a pig. It would be advisable to control him before he becomes a pork dish."

Tong seemed to take it well and replied.

Carmen reported, "He said it would be best not to make trouble here."

I watched Tong bow his head slightly to Chan, and he returned the gesture.

"You okay?" I asked her.

"Yes, fine, thank you, Mr Stone."

As Chan headed my way, I returned to the table, sat down and told Angel, "I think our Mr Chan is a bit more than an actor."

A little while later, after we had all eaten, the band leader made an announcement, "Ladies and gentlemen, we would like to ask Miss Rita Gee and Mr Charlie Chan to come up and sing a duet." Charlie didn't need any persuasion from the others; he was keen to sing. On the other hand, Rita obviously required a little encouragement.

Charlie took the microphone. "Come on up here, Rita, it would be my honour to sing with you."

By now, Vitale had had a few and waved for Rita to take the stage. Rita joined Charlie, and they launched into the Van Morrison classic,

'Moondance.'

Angel leaned closer to me and asked furtively, "So who is Axis Stone anyway?"

"Ah, the red has loosened your tongue, or is it the illuminating company? Axis Stone is a mere vagabond of the world."

"Does that mean he has no home?"

"No, quite the contrary, he calls many places home. But the truth be known, I'm a home on legs."

"That sounds like a silly limerick, Axis Stone lives alone because inside his head he's found his home."

I finished the limerick, "And in that home, he does hide ... waiting for love to come inside."

We held a special moment where through our fixed gaze seemed to pass a thousand years.

"That sounds sad. Please don't go all soppy on me; it has been a nice evening, don't spoil it. I'm reading your mind, Mr Stone, and it's not where I want to go. Tell me, why are you here?"

"To have dinner."

"You're crazy ... I used to know someone who would say things as mad as that. No seriously ... why are you here?"

Behind her through the ceiling to floor windows, I could see the moonlight shimmering like mercury on the calm waters of the Caribbean, adding imagery to Van Morrison's wonderful lyrics. It was at that moment I knew I needed to confide in Angel; she was ready.

"I'm a private detective, Angel. A friend of Roland's recommended me to Roland to look into Richard's disappearance. Coming off a big case, I needed some time away from the Big Apple, and so I popped down to see if I could help."

"That's why Pop gave you Richard's journal?"

"Yes."

"And now you're working me over for more information."

"I wouldn't put it like that, but it's up to you. Look, if I feel I'm getting in the way, I'll just leave and chase some other mystery. It really isn't my style to breeze into a person's life and create waves. I'm an old hippie at heart, and that'd be uncool.

"Am I one of your mysteries to be solved, Mr Stone?"

A silence fell upon us like a shroud while each of us contemplated the conversation.

The light went down low. I leaned across the table and gently kissed her, as Rita sang the Nat King Cole classic, 'When I Fall in Love.'

An awkward expression crossed Angel's face that I read as guilt. She stood, "I've an early start, thank you for dinner. It has been nice."

I watched her leave and then, feeling a little melancholy, watched Charlie and Carmen dancing to the song. They could really cut a formal rug. Then I noticed Angel had stopped in the doorway to also watch Charlie and Carmen. I went over to her.

"Lost something?" I asked.

"Maybe an opportunity."

Tears welled up in her eyes, and she moved off quickly into the lobby. I stayed there watching Charlie and Carmen, thinking about how Angel might be feeling. Then I noticed Tong was asleep in his chair with his mouth wide open. Unwilling to miss a payback opportunity for being punched, I grabbed a bottle of Tabasco from the condiments table, emptied the contents into a glass, added some fresh chili and loads of cracked pepper, and walked menacingly over to Tong. When I reached him, I took the salt shaker from the table, unscrewed the lid, and poured the salt into Tong's open mouth. Then I placed the glass containing the chili concoction on the table in front of him and stepped back to watch. Tong woke abruptly with a horrid thirst, saw the drink in front of him, and immediately gulped it down. His eyes opened to the size of dinner plates—he exhaled as though he'd swallowed hot coals. He grabbed an ice bucket and drank the contents. Pleased with my work, I dusted my hands and ambled off, leaving Tong putting out the fire.

CHAPTER
FOUR

Roland was at his desk reading the morning newspaper when the door opened, and in walked Angel, happy as Larry. "Good morning Pop. Morning Paddy."

With the tabloid still held up, Roland responded, "He won't answer you, dear; he's only a dummy." He lowered the paper. "Now, don't you look like a breath of fresh air."

Angel tapped Paddy on the head and then went to Roland and gave him a peck on the cheek. Then she looked him in the eye, "Why did you give Mr Stone the journal?"

"Well, I thought it might be time to stop sweeping stuff under the carpet. I'm an old man, my dear … and if there is one thing I'd like to see before I go—"

"Wait a minute. Where is this leading? Are you trying your hand at match-making? If you are, you're out of order … I … I—"

"Now calm down, girl. I didn't say anything about romance. I'm talking about the truth behind Richard's disappearance. I know you're loathe to deal with it … but you can't keep it bottled up inside forever. You're young, life has a lot more to offer than what you're taking. Just talk to him about it … He's a good man … and he's on our side."

"I can't, Pop … I just can't," she burst into tears and stormed out of the study.

With a tear in his eye, the old man swivelled on his chair and watched her run like a gazelle down the track towards the jetty. He turned back to Paddy. "Put my big foot in it again, didn't I, Paddy?"

A knock at the door broke the moment. "It's Charlie Chan, sir."

Roland lightened up, "Come in, my boy."

Charlie entered and was startled by Paddy. He bowed to Roland, and they shook hands.

"Pleased to finally meet you, Mr Harris."

"Don't mind Paddy there..."

"It reminds me of a few dummies I've met recently."

"It says a lot about a person's character when they don't address Paddy as a person ... Sit down, lad. Let me look at you. Yes, yes, I can see it. You're the spitting image of your grandfather ... A most sagacious sleuth was old Charlie. You must be proud of your dynasty, my boy."

"I am most honoured that my grandfather's best friend should choose to invite me, a mere novice private detective ... to help him."

"Forget the courtesies; you're a Chan, young man. And if you're only half as good as old Charlie was, you'll do me fine. Now, let me explain why I invited you here. The days I have left on this planet can be counted on the one calendar. But before I have the pleasure of meeting my grand master, I have two issues to resolve. The first is to see my daughter-in-law secure ... and the second is to find my son's remains so that I can finally lay him to rest. Now, you may well ask why I have waited ten years to look for his body. Well, it has taken that long for my Angel to put the trauma of Richard's death behind her ... You see, she holds the key—"

~ ~ ~

Angel was sitting on the end of the pier dangling her legs over the side, contemplating Roland's comment when I came up behind her.

"No matter what way you look at it, the old boy's right."

She swivelled around abruptly to face me.

"Will you stop creeping up on me like that."

I sat beside her with the journal in my hands. "Like I've done this before? Maybe in another life."

"Oh, stop being so nice; I don't want to laugh. Just let me be sad and miserable, will you."

She turned away to conceal her tears.

"Locking trauma away in some dark corner of your mind might not be a healthy solution."

"We all have our ways of dealing with things. What's good for you or Pop might not be good for me. Right?"

Looking out to sea seemed to drown her sorrows. She took a deep breath and after a moment of contemplation, wiped the tears away and faced me.

"I'm sorry."

"I would be too if I had snot hanging out of my nose."

That got a giggle out of her as she wiped her nose with the back of her hand

"You're crazy ... It's a great day. Do you dive?"

"Does that mean going in a boat?"

"Of course, it's the only way to get to the reef."

"But I'm allergic to boats, they make me throw up."

"Look, it's as smooth as a baby's bottom; you won't get seasick, I promise."

I took her at her word, and we got kitted up.

~ ~ ~

Roland heard the Lindos Lady start up and turned to look out the window.

"Ah, good, we have contact. Stone has broken the ice. She's taking him out into her world. The sea."

"I took the liberty of checking our Mr Stone..."

Roland turned back with interest. "Excellent, my boy. Any skeletons?"

"A bit of a mystery man, really."

"He has recently solved a few extremely difficult cases. He is well thought of by the LAPD, the NYPD, and the CIB in Australia. Believe me, that's a good rap for a PI. You know about his folks?"

"Of course, of course, who doesn't, just two of the best crime fiction writers ever."

"Well, let's see. If he can help Angel open up, then that's great, as long as he's not the kind of guy to take advantage of her and cause personal damage, she seems fragile."

"She sure is, but I have a good gut feeling about him. He reminds me a lot of Richard. Same sort of extremist logic … That will certainly attract our Angel. By the way, do you think a fly loops the loop or flips to land upside down on the ceiling?"

Charlie crossed his eyebrows, pondering the conundrum that he figured Holmes might well have proposed to Dr Watson.

~ ~ ~

I completed checking my diving gear and joined Angel at the helm. She removed her hat and shook her long auburn hair out into the warm sea breeze. This was the first time I saw the real Angel; a stunningly natural, beautiful woman.

"Now you're at home," I said, "you're becoming calmer by the second. I can easily see the girl in the woman.

"The sharks out here are easier to recognise, that's all, unlike the ones on land."

She pulled back the throttles and triggered the anchor winch.

Minutes later, we were thirty metres underwater, surrounded by the dazzling splendour of rainbow-like corals and vividly coloured fish. Angel took me to where the reef was under threat from the silt pollution she had spoken of. It was sad to see the devastation: dead bleached coral, vast areas void of life, a veritable ecological graveyard.

~ ~ ~

Later, sitting at the stern of Lindos Lady, we removed our scuba gear. Angel no longer appeared a tomboy out of her wetsuit in her swimsuit.

"That was an experience to be savoured, thank you."

"That's okay, you're a good diver," she said, drying her hair with a towel.

"And you're a stunning lady.

My compliment prompted an unexpected reaction. She suddenly became self-conscious, covered up her body with the towel, and headed for the cabin to change.

"That wasn't a come-on, merely an observation."

I had stopped her at the cabin door, and she reconsidered. "My senses say you're telling the truth, Axis, but…"

"But what? A ghost inside is claiming otherwise?"

She moved inside the cabin, leaving me thinking I had triggered another anxiety attack.

I dried myself off and settled on the gunwale. To my astonishment, Angel appeared from the cabin donning a sarong and a bikini top. Her long hair cascaded gracefully over her soft brown shoulders, making her the embodiment of loveliness and taking my breath away. She fetched two cokes from the cooler, offered one to me, and took a seat beside me.

"Thanks. So, tell me about your gift?"

"You asked me that last night."

"Yeah, but I got no answer."

"I really don't like to talk about it, but—"

She was about to evade the topic but changed her mind. Things were looking up.

"I guess I've always had it … can't be sure, I'm an orphan. Anyhow, when the frequencies are right, you know, in tune, I can lock onto people's thoughts. Just like you do, I guess."

"No, not quite like that. I'm not equipped with extra sensory perception, just sharpened evaluation techniques I think I picked up from my folks. Do you channel or have visions?"

"Like premonitions? Yes … But mostly I have the wildest dreams."

"What kind of dreams? Not dirty, I hope."

"Ha! None that I care to share with you. No, I've had a recurring dream ever since I can remember. I clearly see myself, but in a different place and time in history ... long, long ago, mostly. I feel it's a past life regression, a connection of body and mind ... I don't know why I'm telling you this, I hardly even know you and—"

"It's alright ... think of it as friendship bonding ... seems like you're pretty informed."

"Yes, I'm not one for the internet, too much rubbish to wade through, but I read a lot. Funny, I'm always the woman with a quest to save a tribe or the world or something. I always meet the same man, I love him, but I've never actually seen his face. So often he's there. I can feel him, but we never seem to get together. Because I see him—"

She seemed to drift off into some kind of catatonic stupor. "See him what...? Angel? ... Knock, knock, hello, are you there?"

She suddenly snapped out of her reverie and said to my amazement, "Killed ... I see, or at least I know that he's killed, in lots of different ways ... over and over again."

"Killed? Whoa, that's pretty morbid. Do you think you're on some kind of quest?"

"I've never thought of it like that ... but, yes, maybe ... well sometimes."

"You need to read 'The White Goddess' by Robert Graves."

She stood and then moved about as if on a cloud—she seemed to gather her thoughts and said, "Richard was a lot like you. He had a quest to seek the truth. That's probably what got him killed. I was only 18 at the time ... we were just married ... I came here at 17 to work as a trainee maid. I didn't speak good English. Richard and Pop taught me everything. I loved Richard from the very moment I first met him but he was the son of the boss, and I didn't think I stood a chance of being his girl." She explained, fighting back tears. "Richard was born here and spoke the local language. His mother was a local. She died giving birth to him. Pop was a great father. A man with a totally open mind and a real love for this his adopted country and its people. He came here with the forces ... Something of a local hero is our Major Roland B. Harris ... Ever since he was a child, Richard loved exploring. He'd explored every centimetre of San Pedro, underwater, on land, you name it, he'd covered it. For some reason, he believed that there was a secret to be found. Remnants of a lost civilization, a place where some sort of key to the future was buried. A year before we met, he had found a ruin in the mountains. It was his Shangri-La or Eldorado. He was excavating it when he disappeared. For a long time, I expected him to just walk out of the jungle one day and say, 'Hi princess, did you miss me?'"

She broke down. I embraced her and let her cry on my shoulder. It was a release for her to finally be free of some of the history that had been eating away at her.

"It's alright, let it all out. You'll feel better."

She withdrew from my embrace and began pacing about, deep in thought, her knuckle firmly between her teeth.

I allowed her some time to regain her composure, and then, when I thought the moment was right, I asked, "Was anyone with him when he disappeared?"

"No. But..." Emotion was building again. "That day he asked me to go with him and, and ... I didn't." Again, she burst into tears.

"Why not? ... Angel, why not?" I needed to push her to reveal the truth. I could feel it was a dim, dark secret, the cause of her guilt.

She calmed a little, sat, and, wringing her hands, admitted, "I ... I told him I had to take guests for a dive and—"

"But it was a lie."

She nodded, the tears flowing. "Before Richard and I started our relationship, I had met a guy."

"Your boyfriend."

"Yes, but we had split up ... it was all over. God, I was only sixteen. Well, he had tracked me down here. He threatened to tell Richard about us if I didn't meet him .... I had to meet him, I had no choice ... My God, if I had been with Richard, he wouldn't be dead!"

I stood and embraced her again; this time, she melted into my arms.

"Shush, shush, It's okay … It's out now, you're not to blame. It was destiny."

She pulled away and looked into my eyes. "Pop must never know about Mike. It would kill him. I shouldn't have been with him that day. Promise me you won't tell him."

"I promise. Sit down now … take a deep breath. Feel the calmness around you."

She sat and did as I asked while gazing at the calm blue sea.

"Did you ever see the ruin?"

"Yes, I helped him dig a couple of times."

"His journal mentions a treasure. Was that what he was after?"

"He was so secretive about what it was, but I could sense it wasn't money. It was knowledge. He did mention treasure once or twice and a book, a manuscript I think … I can't remember … Is that what you want, treasure?"

"No, not at all. Angel, you need to take me to the ruin."

An eternity seemed to pass. Then she looked at me with a resolute expression and muttered, "Okay, I will."

CHAPTER
FIVE

Vitale was pacing the jetty like an angry bear. Rita sat on a crate, calmly filing her fingernails, and Tong stood like a lighthouse, gazing out to sea.

"She should have been here an hour ago! Where the hell is she?" Vitale growled.

"I don't know why you're getting so worked up; we've got nothing but time on our hands. She'll be here. Just enjoy the salinity," Rita responded.

"Great English, babe, that's serenity ... salinity is the salt in the ocean."

"Well, there's plenty of that here, isn't there?" she returned serve.

"I'm surrounded by mental re-treads. Come on, Tong, let's get some lunch. We'll leave Rita to her 'salinity.'"

Rita pulled a funny face when he turned his back, then resumed filing her nails. While Tong and Vitale were walking the wharf toward the hotel, she looked out to sea and spotted the Lindos Lady on the horizon, and grumbled to herself, "See? Didn't listen. Never listens—big know-it-all, narcissistic ignoramus."

~ ~ ~

Charlie was sat under a palm tree in the lotus position, meditating. Carmen, scantily clad, was beside him, sipping from a coconut and swaying to a tune playing on her iPhone.

Vitale and Tong walked past … Vitale glanced at Charlie.

"Look, there's another mental re-tread."

Though Charlie was within earshot, he kept his eyes closed and quipped, "Phew, can I smell fresh bull crap?"

Tong had to restrain Vitale, who growled like a rabid dog at Charlie's remark. "Why, I'll…"

As they moved off, Carmen removed her earbuds and said, "Boss, mind if I take a swim?"

Still with his eyes closed, meditating, Charlie replied, "Go right ahead."

She got up and headed toward the hotel to change.

When Carmen entered the hotel lobby, Vitale was taking out his frustration on Boy, with Tong standing behind like a monument.

"So, get her on the freaking radio and find out where the hell she is, idiot! I had a booking for 9.30 A.M., it's now midday!"

Boy looked rattled. "Yes, sir, I'm sorry, Mr Vitale."

"Useless half-wit! Argh! Another re-tread. What did I tell you, Tong? I'm surrounded!"

Boy disappeared into the back office, and Vitale turned from the desk fuming. He caught Carmen by the arm as she was walking past and pulled her to him. She struggled to get away, and he groped at her backside.

"I believe you're taking unfair advantage of the lady, Mr Bull." Charlie moved in but was stopped by Tong's vice-like grip. "My dispute is not with you, Tong. Let me go."

Tong tightened his grip. Charlie let fly at Tong with a flurry of martial arts blows and knocked Tong backward, hard, against the front desk.

Impressed by Charlie's martial prowess, Vitale freed Carmen.

"You handle yourself pretty well for an actor," Vitale growled.

Still shaped up and ready for more, Charlie said, "Yes, but unlike you, I do my own stunts. Pull another one like that, and I'll have you for breakfast … egg."

"First, it was bull, now it's egg. You know, I've been looking in mirrors since you were in your father's nuts, and I've never seen a friggin' bull or an egg ... So what is it wit you, huh? Need glasses? You should be really careful who you're threatening, Chinaman. You might just become a permanent resident with your own little plot here."

"Plots don't frighten me, pal, I'm an actor."

Vitale reached out sharply and grabbed Carmen by the hair, pulling her toward him viciously.

"Yeah! Well, let me put you in the picture, wise ass ... Take him, Tong!"

Tong had been taking it easy and laid into Charlie. A powerful right sent Charlie smashing bodily through the front window. Vitale irreverently pushed Carmen aside.

"You're too skinny for me anyway, bitch. Come on, Tong," Vitale spat like a viper, and they moved off to the dining room. Carmen helped Charlie to his feet.

"Are you alright, boss? That certainly wasn't in the job description."

"You're right," Charlie said, wiping his bloody eyebrow. They both looked around at the sound of a vehicle pulling up on the forecourt. It was a black stretch limousine.

A dapper-looking businessman accompanied by a surly-looking gangster-type stepped out of the vehicle and entered the hotel, carrying briefcases. They looked very suspicious to Charlie.

The businessman glanced at the broken glass crunching under his shoes, nodded to Carmen, and then to Charlie before going to the front desk.

As Carmen helped Charlie up the staircase, gripping his aching back, he said, "So, the plot thickens with new cast members."

"Who do you suppose they are?"

"Instinct and observation suggest; the smaller man dresses sharply like a real estate developer but nodded like a politician when talking to Boy ... car salesmen do these things too but are always looking about, as he does, for recognition. He wears a Patek Philippe watch, which few of those professions could afford; most would choose a Rolex to impress—better known. He acts like all of the above, so I would conclude he's probably a crook. The guy with him, I suspect, is his bodyguard."

"Wow ... That's impressive. I knew they were crooks as soon as they got out of the limo."

Charlie stopped her at the landing and asked, "How's that?"

"They're both wearing guns."

Charlie had been shot down by his novice. "You go ahead to the room, log on. I'll be there in a moment."

"What about my swim?"

"Was that in the job description?" He questioned facetiously, and then peeked around the corner down to the lobby below. Boy was directing the new arrivals to the dining room. They moved off. Holding his back, Charlie stealthily descended the staircase and confronted Boy cleaning up the broken glass.

"Sorry about the mess, Boy," he said then quickly put his finger to his lips to hush him, and then asked quietly, "Who are they?"

Boy whispered, "The big dollar dresser is a fat real estate developer named Raman. He is also running for mayor. I don't know the other one. They're here to see Mr Vitale."

"Get me a bottle of Vitale's favourite wine. I'll be back in a moment." He hurried as fast as his sore back would permit and ascended the staircase.

A few minutes later, Charlie and Carmen were in their room, surrounded by an excessive amount of luggage. The door was open, and Rita, passing by, stopped to peek in.

"Hey, welcome to Fantasy Island. I enjoyed our duet last night."

Charlie approached her, saying, "Rita, I had the pleasure of seeing you perform in L.A. a few years ago."

Carmen let out a fake cough, signalling Charlie to end the flirtatious conversation. Rita looked past Charlie at Carmen and raised her eyebrows.

"I hope we can do it again sometime, Rita," Charlie said, turning on the charm before closing the door.

"Rita is about as subtle as Delilah opening a hair salon called Samson's," Carmen commented, her jealousy evident.

Charlie chuckled. "That's very good, Carmen; Samson's. Rita is quite harmless."

Wearing glasses, Carmen was a far cry from the airhead persona she had presented publicly. There was no hint of that character now.

"Okay, let's get to work," Charlie said firmly. "Log on and research Raman, a local developer who, believe it or not, is running for mayor."

While Carmen typed away on her laptop, Charlie opened a briefcase and retrieved a folder filled with documents. Beneath the papers, he found a .357 magnum pistol.

Carmen looked up at Charlie, who was holding the pistol. "Mr Chan, I need to point out that my job description didn't include sharing the same bed."

Charlie walked over to a connecting door and opened it. "Here is your room, as per our contract."

Carmen raised a single eyebrow above the rim of her glasses, showing a hint of scepticism in her expression. Charlie returned to his briefcase and took out a small device. He extended an antenna from the side of the case and flicked a switch to activate a recording device. Speaking into the device, he said, "One two, one two." He adjusted the recording level and then, with the device in hand, headed for the door. "I'll be back."

Charlie, no longer bothered by his back pain, swiftly descended the stairs to the front counter. Boy was there, clearly intrigued by the unfolding intrigue. Charlie took the bottle of wine from him and discreetly attached the tiny bugging device to its base.

I entered the scene and noticed the broken window, then I overheard Charlie inform Boy quietly, "Take this to Vitale. When he's done with it, leave it on the table, alright?"

Boy nodded in agreement.

"Oh, and don't discard it later. Keep it for me, okay?"

"I'll keep it for you. I've seen this in Bond James 007 movies," Boy remarked.

I sensed what was happening and teased Charlie, "Following in the footsteps of your famous namesake, Chan?"

Boy went off to deliver the wine, and Charlie started to ascend the stairs. Turning back, he added with a playful, broken English Chinese accent, "Eventually, the smoke clears, oh honourable acquaintance."

"Was Confucius a relative as well?" I retorted with a grin.

When Charlie entered the room, Carmen was completely engrossed in the bugged conversation between Vitale and Raman that she was monitoring. Charlie sat on the edge of the bed to listen.

"So, what's it going to take for the old man to sell?"

"That's Raman," Charlie told Carmen.

"I told you before he won't sell."

"And that's Vitale ... the plot thickens," Charlie said.

Raman said angrily, "I didn't ask you that! What will it take? You've already been here two weeks, Vinny, you said it would be done in a couple of days. Do I need to remind you what's at stake here and who's paying the bills? I have contractors on hold, costing me a fortune, and that's on top of your overinflated fee ... now, get off your ass."

"Alright, alright, keep your shirt on. I know the statistics; I just have to find the right button, right? The daughter-in-law inherits the lot."

"So what do you plan to do about that?"

"What? Do you think I'm stupid?"

There was static, and Charlie said, "He's moved the bottle of wine."

Vitale called out, "Boy, Boy, more wine. Tong, go get the idiot ... and here ... take the dead marine with you. Now where were we...?"

Carmen and Charlie listened to Tong's footsteps as he carried the empty wine bottle to the bar to find Boy. Charlie turned off the recorder. "Hmm, just when it was getting interesting. It sounds bad. Big money going out with Roland being stubborn, unwilling to sell ... A fee for Vitale to close the deal ... it's likely to get nasty. What was on the database about Raman?"

"Nothing. Mostly access denied."

"Hmm, he must have paid to have a shady record erased. Got to look clean if you want to be mayor. Check the company register to see who he's in business with."

As Carmen typed, she snarled, "All politicians are corrupt."

"Not all, but like anywhere in the world, there are some bad apples among the good ones." He fetched another bug from his briefcase and tuned it to the recorder/player. "One two, one two ... I'll be back."

"I'm sure you will?"

He went to the window, opened it, and looked back at her quizzically. "Why do you keep saying that?"

Without looking up from typing, she said, "Because you keep saying you'll be back."

"You're right ... I'll return."

To Carmen's surprise, he climbed out of the window.

"I'm sure you will," she muttered to herself.

CHAPTER
SIX

Charlie stealthily entered Vitale's room, noticing it was far more spacious than his own—a luxurious suite. He surveyed the area, seeking the perfect spot to conceal the bug. After contemplation, he opted to hide it beneath the ink blotter on the writing desk. Suddenly, the sound of keys rattling at the door reached his ears. With no time to retreat through the window, he hastily squeezed into the wardrobe and pulled the door closed.

Peering through the door's louvres, he kept a vigilant eye on Rita as she entered the room. She headed toward a chest of drawers, opened the topmost drawer, extracted a flask of liquor, and took an anxious swig. Her resolve bolstered by the alcohol, she proceeded to undress for a shower. Humming to herself, she assessed her reflection in the wardrobe's mirror.

Meanwhile, in Charlie's room, Carmen monitored the bug's transmissions and heard Rita's singing. Then, she heard Rita remark, "You know, for my age, I'm still alluring. My boobs have sagged a tad, but I've still got the legs of a dancer—ones Madonna would envy."

Believing the conversation was with Charlie, Carmen angrily removed her glasses, her irritation mounting.

After a brief dance in front of the mirror, Rita made her way to the bathroom. With hesitation, Charlie cautiously nudged open the wardrobe door, intending to make a swift exit. However, just as he was about to slip away, Rita unexpectedly reappeared from the bathroom, catching him red-handed. In shock, she hurriedly covered herself with a towel. Then, her demeanour shifted from surprise to flirtatious.

"Charlie..."

All Charlie desired was a swift exit from the situation. She gracefully approached him, encircling her arms around his neck, and let the towel fall to the floor.

Just then, they both heard a key turning in the door. Rita's panic surged, and she hastily retrieved the fallen towel to wrap it around herself. "Shit! It's Vinny, quick!"

She urged Charlie back into the wardrobe and swiftly slipped into the bathroom.

Vinny entered with Tong, Raman, and Dino, Raman's bodyguard.

"Take a seat," Vitale instructed them. "I didn't want to talk with that fuckin' Indiana Jones clone sitting a table away all ears."

"Who is he anyway?" Raman inquired.

"I dunno, some friend of the old boy's, Axis Stone or something."

"If you had asked me to take care of the old man ... it would have been done by now," Dino grumbled.

Vitale snapped, drew a .38, and pressed it against Dino's temple. With a malevolent grin, he stared at Dino and cocked the trigger. Vitale revelled in his role as a seasoned gangster. "You've got quite a mouth on you, pal ... No-one asked for you freaking opinion, got it?" he snarled into the larger man's ear.

"Alright, alright, chill, Vinny, we're on the same side here. Put the piece away before someone gets hurt," Raman said diplomatically.

Like a child who had thrown a tantrum and got what he wanted, Vitale gradually composed himself and holstered the gun.

In the closet, Charlie had beads of sweat trickling down his cheeks. The shadow cast by the louvres gave him the appearance of a prisoner, albeit with horizontal bars. Through the louvres, he observed Vitale pacing restlessly like an agitated cat. The sound of Rita singing a snippet of 'Moondance' emanated from the bathroom.

"Rita!" Vitale called out.

"No, it's the maid. Thought I'd take a shower while I'm cleaning," she shouted back in jest.

"Wise ass. Yeah, Rita, very funny—who writes your lines, can't be you, you can't write! Shut up will ya, I've got guests here."

Raman was almost in hysterics at the banter between the pair of them. "Vinny, Vinny... Ah," he said, wiping the tears of laughter from his eyes. "I had no idea Rita was a comedian as well ... You guys are the funniest double act since Lucille Ball and Desi Arnaz."

Rita hadn't heard about the guests and stepped out of the bathroom naked and wet, her hair wrapped in a towel. When she saw the three men sitting on the lounge, gobsmacked, she simply smiled at them and then casually returned to the bathroom, humming 'Moondance' to herself, totally unaffected.

Dino was mind-blown, his cigar drooping from his lips. Raman was unable to contain himself and almost fell off the chair with laughter. Tong was stone-faced. Vitale was just shaking his head.

In the wardrobe, Charlie had to cover his mouth to suppress his laughter.

"Damn exhibitionist," Vitale grumbled. "Always putting on a show, aren't you, Rita?"

Rita called from the bathroom, "Hey, I'd like to get dressed. How about you and your buddies take a hike and give a girl some privacy."

Carmen couldn't believe what she was hearing. She finally realised that Charlie must be trapped in Vitale's room. "Oh, poor Charlie," she muttered to herself.

"She's no comedian; she's the village idiot," Vitale said, then yelled back to her, "No, Rita ... you can just park your ass in there until we're finished here." He looked back at Raman. "Now, where were we?"

"You bastard!" Rita shrieked.

Vitale ignored her.

Raman spoke up, "I'll leave Dino here for a couple of days, no longer ... I'll drive back to town and expect results in—"

He was stopped by the sound of fists pounding on the wall.

Vitale was incensed and yelled at the wall, "Who the hell is that?"

The muffled sound of Carmen's voice responded, "Will you shut up in there? I can hear every word you say."

With an astonished look on his face, Vitale turned to Raman, "Jesus, now even the walls have ears." He turned back to the wall and yelled, "Alright, lady! Just chill."

Raman stood, and put his suitcoat around his shoulders, with putting his arms through the sleeves—gangster style, "Down to the bar, I need a drink. Maybe Indiana Jones has gone on crusade."

"Yeah, I hope it's his last."

Charlie watched them leave, and then, after a few seconds, Rita emerged from the bathroom wrapped in a towel. As Charlie stepped out of the wardrobe in a ball of sweat, she posed as if for the front cover of Vogue magazine.

"Did I hear mention of a drink? You're a naughty boy, Charlie Chan. Now get out of here so I can change."

Charlie made for the window.

Hearing Charlie returning, Carmen met him at the window and extended a helping hand.

"Thanks for the wall-pounding distraction. I was in the wardrobe; damn hot in there," Charlie admitted with a sigh.

"Now, that was in the job description," she joked. "Listen, I downloaded a report on Raman's company and the shareholders."

Angel stopped by the front desk to speak with Boy, who was eager to share his '007 experience' with Charlie. However, he had a warning for her first.

"Angel, Mr Vitale was furious about you being late for his charter."

Angel responded nonchalantly, "Oh well, shit happens."

Boy wasn't done; he held up a bottle of wine like it was a precious treasure and said, "And that's not all you missed, look at this!"

Angel raised an eyebrow, "Have you been drinking on the job, Boy? Tell me later; I need to see Pop about something."

Boy complained as she left, "But it's 007!"

When Angel entered Roland's office, she found him asleep at his desk. She decided to play a little trick on him and quietly sneaked up, planting a kiss on his forehead. She then made her way towards the door, almost making her escape.

But Roland suddenly spoke, "A good trick pretending to be asleep. Pretty girls sneak up and kiss you. Wish I'd known the trick fifty years ago."

She laughed and rushed back to give him a warm hug. However, as she touched him, she experienced a sudden, vivid vision. Bright light blinded her, and in her mind's eye, she saw Roland's walking stick falling to the ground, his legs buckling. Another flash, and the vision ended. It was a premonition, and it left her visibly troubled.

Roland, sensing her distress, asked, "Are you alright? You look pale."

Angel held her chest as if trying to calm her racing heart. She replied, "Yes, yes, it's just been ... um," unable to find the words to explain her vision, she decided not to elaborate further. "Pop, in the morning, I'm going to take Axis to the ruin."

Roland responded, "I'm glad ... If this keeps up, lassie, I'll die a happy man."

Angel stared at him, still shaken by the vision of his demise. She pleaded, "Don't say things like that, Pop. Don't tempt fate. I've told you about that before!"

Struggling to get up, Roland collected his walking sticks with Angel's help, and they headed for the door. However, he stopped for a moment, giving her a knowing look. "Sometimes your second sight worries me, Lassie."

She tried to lighten the mood with a smile, saying, "It worries you? What about me? Anyhow, it isn't always right. How many times have I said we were going to catch a big fish, and we don't?"

They exchanged a loving look, and she admitted, "I love you, Pop."

With a playful tone, he replied, "Sorry, lassie. I'm old enough to be your father. Best to try someone a wee bit younger. What about Paddy here?"

They both laughed, sharing a moment of warmth and affection.

~ ~ ~

That evening, in blue and white pinstriped pyjamas, Charlie was lounging on his bed, engrossed in reading the newspaper. Carmen entered the room, dressed in a see-through negligee, and strategically positioned herself in the doorway, allowing the backlight to accentuate the transparency of her outfit.

"Goodnight, Mr Chan," she purred seductively.

Without lowering the newspaper, Charlie replied indifferently, "Goodnight, Carmen."

Hoping to capture his attention, Carmen inquired, "So, what's the plan for tomorrow?"

Charlie, still immersed in the newspaper, casually responded, "We'll just take it as it comes."

Slightly disappointed, Carmen turned to go through the connecting door. However, Charlie lowered the newspaper and peered at her over his reading glasses, a hint of intrigue in his eyes. He put the paper aside.

"Oh, Carmen."

Her face brightened, and she gracefully glided over to him. Just as she was leaning in for a kiss, a loud 'bang' echoed through the room, startling them both. The sound came from the bug monitor.

Charlie sat up straight, excitement coursing through him. "That was the door to Vitale's room closing; they're back."

Realising that the romantic moment had been overtaken by events, Carmen forlornly moved away and retreated to her own bedroom. Charlie settled in an armchair next to his briefcase and listened intently to the bug.

"I should've known better than to bring you along on a business trip. You're nothing but a cheap drunk," Vitale's voice snarled.

"So, what's this? Now the party's over, you think you can dump all your frustration on me? Well, forget it, baby. I don't want it. Keep it all for yourself," Rita retorted defiantly.

"I'll teach you some respect," Vitale threatened.

Charlie winced at the sound of a loud slap, indicating that Vitale had physically struck her. Rita continued her retort, "You gotta earn respect, Vinny ... One day I'm gonna walk right out on you..." Her voice broke into sobs.

"Ha! Now you're being a freakin' comedian again," Vitale scoffed.

The bug picked up more sounds of physical violence, more screams. Charlie had heard enough. He turned off the device, looked around, and realised Carmen had left the room. He sighed, turned out the light, and settled in for the night.

CHAPTER
SEVEN

The sun was just about to peep over the horizon. I stood at the front desk, waiting for Angel, who arrived dressed in jungle greens.

"Good morning. How are you feeling, up for it?" I asked her.

"Yep, it's going to be an eventful day. We'll take the jeep."

The open cab US Army Jeep sped under Angel's control along a dirt jungle track. We had to shout to be heard above the engine noise and the sound of the tyres on the bumpy road.

"How the hell did he find this place?"

"Like I told you. He explored every inch of the country around here. Beautiful, don't you think?"

I looked at her. "Yeah, stunning."

"The only thing keeping it from being turned into chopsticks and toothpicks is Pop."

"How's that?"

"As far as the eye can see, all the way to the mountains over there ... is under perpetual lease. The Lindos estate; The beautiful estate. 'Lindos' is 'beautiful' in Spanish."

"Must be worth zillions."

"On paper maybe, but not cash. We're almost broke."

The road ended at the foot of the mountains. Angel pulled the jeep into a clearing and stopped. She leaned her head on the steering wheel, disturbed. I was already out of the jeep, looking around.

I looked back at her, it was obvious she was having trouble. "You okay?"

"No. I can't do this, Axis. I can feel Richard's presence ... It's unnerving. Let's go ... Maybe some other time." She started the engine.

I moved around to her side of the jeep, reached in, switched off the engine, and held out my hand. After a moment's contemplation, she reluctantly took it, and I helped her out. I held her by the shoulders and gazed into her eyes.

"I understand what you're going through ... it's to be expected."

"Axis, really, I—"

"Shush. Trust me ... You don't know me from Adam, but I know I can help you ... and only because I want to. But I can only help you if you're prepared to help yourself. Do you want to change the way you are feeling?"

"Yes, more than anything. It's like carrying around so much emotional baggage."

"Good, then it's time for a little de-enmeshing."

"I don't think I can..."

"Just trust me ... You have visions as well as second sight, right?"

"Sometimes ... but I don't—"

"Right. Now, I want you to take off your boots and socks."

She reluctantly followed my instructions. I was speaking in an almost hypnotic tone, something I'd learned from a Chinese masseuse a while back who was into tantric Zen.

"Right. Feel the earth beneath your feet? Let its energy flow into your body to calm you. Concentrate. Breathe deep breaths, in through your nose, out through your mouth ... that's good. Now, with your hands, form the outline of Richard standing in front of you ... form him in every detail ... now, make him materialise."

She could see a ghost-like image of Richard standing in front of her.

"You see him?"

"Yes."

"Fine, now, visualise the energy flowing between you and Richard."

I could vaguely see it myself, manifested in the air, but I knew to her it was much more vivid.

"Can you see where the energy is flowing from and its direction?"

"Yes, it's all flowing from me into Richard."

"That's right, good. Now, I want you to turn and face away from Richard."

She complied.

"Now, using your finger, make an image of yourself in the air ... the perfect you. The illuminated you, your higher-self."

While Richard's image remained, Angel created another ghost, this time of herself ... her own aura now changed to a different colour from her clone.

"Can you see her?"

"Yes, I can."

"Good, now turn back to Richard and create a second image of Richard ... his higher-self."

She did it, and now there were two images of each of them floating in the air, ghostly apparitions.

"So, make the energy that is channelling between you and Richard instead channel between Richard and his higher-self."

The energy flow was now directed from her through the first image of Richard into the second.

"Right, now using your hand, shut off the energy from you to Richard."

She swept her hand through the air and severed the flow of energy. The energy field vanished but continued between the two Richards. She was sobbing because she could feel the love leaving her with that energy.

"Can you see how the energy is still connected between Richard and his higher self? Now turn back to your higher-self and send that energy to her."

Still sobbing, she obeyed, and her higher-self began to glow. The auras now matched in colour hue.

"The love you have for Richard you are now giving to yourself. Feel how warm that love is to yourself."

"I feel it."

"Now turn back to Richard. See how he's in touch with himself?"

She did it and nodded.

"Good, now ... let him go."

The two images of Richard faded, and then the energy that remained suddenly dissolved skyward. I waited a moment, then placed my open palms on her back as Angel and her higher-self merged into one.

"It's over. How do you feel?" I asked gently.

She was quietly sobbing. "I, I feel a great sense of sadness ... freedom ... and love."

"Do you feel a sense of loss?" I asked.

She thought for a long moment, then said, "Yes, I do, but I feel happy. I have released his love, haven't I?"

"Yes, you have. Well done. Now you can become that higher-self. You have the love for yourself that you've always needed. Let's sit down for a moment and feel nature flow through us before we move on."

~ ~ ~

Charlie and Carmen were having breakfast on the porch with Roland and Boy.

"Why didn't you tell me these gangsters are trying to buy you out?" Charlie asked.

Roland pulled a smug look and said, "Well, a wise old Chinaman once told me; sometimes it is best to hear the story of the race from the horse's mouth."

"That would have been my Grandfather, but these are gangsters, not horses, Mr Harris," Charlie said with a stern look.

"Yes, yes, you're of course correct Charlie. I am a silly old fool to test you ... So, you say this tape recording suggests these scoundrels will resort to violence to take Lindos from me?"

"It certainly sounds that way to me."

"What do you propose, my boy?"

Boy thought the question was directed at him and proposed, "Well, we can't call the police; they would have been paid off."

Charlie let it go and asked, "Where's your daughter-in-law, Angel?"

"She has taken Mr Stone to the ruins," Roland said happily.

Charlie reclined in his seat, thinking. "Hmm."

"You're not suggesting that he's implicated, are you?"

"No. Not by Vitale's Indiana Jones comment ... No, I'm just concerned for her safety..."

"By the look in their eyes yesterday ... I'd say it's more her chastity that might be under threat," Carmen said smugly.

"Do you suspect they might try to use Angel to get me to sign over?"

"Maybe as ransom..." Charlie suggested gloomily. "Carmen, maybe you could try and get close to Rita. We know she's unhappy; she might just give us a hint as to what's going on."

"I can try. But you know I'm not much of a drinker."

"Boy," Charlie changed focus, "tell Cora to keep her eyes and ears open. The first sign of a move from them and we must be ready to act."

"While at peace, prepare for war," Boy quoted.

"You've got it, son. But we must be very careful. We are dealing with very bad types here, and I don't want anyone hurt," Roland said firmly.

~ ~ ~

Angel was leading me through dense jungle. We stopped at a wide track where a tree had been felled.

"This wasn't here before? Looks like a large piece of machinery has passed through," Angel said.

"Yeah, but quite a while ago, judging by the extent of the

undergrowth," I observed.

"Come on, it's not much further," she said noticing I was sweating up a soup and looking quite knackered.

We followed the track. Within a few minutes, I began to notice a number of large megalithic stone blocks scattered about within the thick undergrowth. Angel stopped, squatted on her haunches, and stabbed her machete into the ground. She took a drink from her water bottle, then handed it to me.

"Well, here we are," she said languidly. "But it has all been flattened. These stone blocks were standing when I was last here, just like a regular lost city."

"That was ten years ago…" I said turning around in a slow circle, struck by the enormity of the desecration. Megalithic stone structures overgrown with vines and lush tropical vegetation had been cast indiscriminately about, like they were worthless props left over from a film set. They appeared to have been pushed over by a bulldozer or some other piece of large machinery.

"Damn them! The entire site has been razed ... and look, they've used explosives to ensure little has survived. Why, Goddamn them? This place must have been awesome when you saw it intact."

"Words cannot capture ... it was exquisite. Are you okay? You look—"

"Not really. Sometimes the ignorance of man totally pisses me off."

"Come on. A little farther, we might get lucky."

We navigated among the massive fallen stones, eventually reaching the base of the mountains. Angel led me through a narrow gorge when she exclaimed, "Yes! It's still here!"

Before us stood a temple carved into the living mountain. Enormous granite blocks formed the facade, fitting together with astonishing precision. I was awestruck.

"It's magnificent. It appears pre-Columbian. Similar megaliths can be found in South America and on certain Pacific islands. Where was he excavating?"

Angel entered the temple, paused, and said, "Somewhere around here. Wait, there ... a tunnel, it's still here. Phew, I need to sit down and catch my breath. Let's just take five."

I watched her approach a large stone sphere, and suddenly, she disappeared down a hole in the ground. I rushed over and peered into the dark chasm, resembling a well.

"Angel ... are you alright?" My voice echoed. No response, I figured it was deep. I quickly retrieved a torch from my kit bag and shined it down the well. I spotted Angel at the bottom of what I estimated to be a twenty-metre shaft, sprawled out and unconscious.

I retrieved a length of rope from my bag, secured one end to a pillar, and tossed the other end down the shaft. With my kit bag slung over my shoulder and the torch clenched between my teeth, I descended into the abyss.

Reaching the end of the rope, I still had two or three metres to go, so I let go and aimed to avoid landing on Angel.

She was unconscious. I swept the torch around and found the decomposed remains of a human body. After examination, I concluded, "Mr Richard Harris, I presume."

Angel stirred. I splashed water from a flask onto her face, reviving her.

"Hey there ... testing. How many fingers am I holding up?" I inquired.

"None," she grumbled.

"Good," I concurred, helping her sit up. "Take it easy. Any injuries?"

"Only my pride," she chuckled. "Must've landed on my butt. Luckily, there's plenty of padding."

I directed the torchlight at the corpse. "I believe we've found your husband."

Angel crawled closer to examine it, her gaze fixed on the remains. She removed the wedding ring from the withered finger of the corpse and gently pressed it to her chest ... shock accompanied the confirmation.

"Oh Richard, I'm so, so sorry, I should've..." she began. I let her have her moment; she needed to express her grief. I examined Richard's skull and discovered a large hole at the back of it. I illuminated the walls of the well, searching for what might have caused the skull injury upon impact, but found nothing.

Angel had regained composure, so I said, "Angel, look at the skull injury."

"It must have happened when he hit the bottom."

"I'm not sure; there's no sign of him struggling to escape ... it appears more like blunt force trauma. He might have already been deceased when he landed here."

I shined the torch and noticed a tunnel leading into a dark abyss. I turned it back toward Angel; she was stowing the wedding ring in her pocket.

"You okay?" I asked.

"Yes, I'll be alright."

"Feel like checking out this tunnel?"

She nodded and concurred with a hint of uncertainty. I led the way into the narrow tunnel, and after a brief hike, we reached a dead end.

"Well, no treasure and no manuscript here." I began to turn back, but Angel still stared at the end wall, as if lost in thought. I waved my hand before her eyes, attempting to snap her out of it. "Hello? Testing..." I was concerned she might be in shock.

"There's something on the other side of this wall," she murmured.

"Are you receiving a psychic message? If you are, stay with it," I urged.

I felt a small mound on the floor with my foot, bent down, and touched it. "Alright..." I retrieved a cigarette lighter from my pocket, took a coin, and wedged it in the lighter to keep the flame burning. With Angel watching with fascination, I carefully positioned the lighter in front of the mound ... it was all intuitive thinking— guesswork mainly.

The light from the open flame suddenly gleamed off a small

crystal embedded in the mound, creating a laser-like beam that struck the end wall. The beam then hit another tiny crystal embedded in the wall, reflecting and bouncing off multiple crystals within the small cavern. Each time it hit a crystal, it remained illuminated, gradually forming a pattern. We examined it, and I said, "It's a pentagram."

"How did you know to do that?" Angel asked, astonished.

"I have no idea. But I don't believe the Ancients were as uninformed as some people might think..."

The red hue of the pentagram abruptly shifted to a brilliant green. I swiftly removed my baseball cap.

"Whoa!" I exclaimed loudly and tossed my cap at the pentagram, "Get down! Now!"

The moment the cap disrupted the beam, a small dart shot out from an inconspicuous hole in the end wall like a missile, whizzing over our heads—a concealed trap. I hastily grabbed the lighter, turned it off, and the pentagram deactivated. I had to juggle the still-hot lighter.

Angel rose to her feet and, seemingly guided by some higher force, approached the end wall. She inserted her thumb into the small hole from which the dart had emerged, and her two fingers into two other holes, as if she were holding a bowling ball. Then, she pulled. A pyramidal-shaped stone emerged from the wall; she rotated it, and the wall clicked, opening.

I restrained Angel from entering, pushed the stone door farther, and shone the torchlight inside. The dusty beam illuminated a large, heavily cobweb-covered chamber. I stepped inside with Angel following closely behind.

CHAPTER EIGHT

The room appeared empty, except for something at the far end that glistened in the torchlight.

"There," Angel pointed out.

We approached cautiously and soon recognised it as a sarcophagus resting atop a stone pedestal, expertly carved from rock. I wiped away the accumulated dust from the lid. "It's made of metal ... and there are hieroglyphs." Retrieving my phone, I captured photographs from various angles. "We might be able to decipher this back at the hotel."

"Open it," Angel insisted.

"No, we can't; exposing it to the air might damage whatever is inside."

"Open it! It's what we're here for. I know it." Her eyes held a profound connection with the sarcophagus, as if on a metaphysical level.

"It's your decision, Angel."

"This was all meant to happen. I just know it."

I held the torch as Angel unfolded a Swiss army knife. With determination, she attempted to pry open the casket. A distinct hiss filled the chamber as the vacuum seal broke. I glanced at Angel; the moment of truth had arrived.

"Well, here's luck, kiddo." I struggled to lift the heavy lid. Once I managed to open it, Angel directed the torchlight inside, and we were immediately struck by the contents. I peered closer; a mummified corpse lay before us. Although the face was concealed by an intricately painted, lifelike death mask, there was no mistaking the resemblance—it was Angel's face!

"It looks like you," I managed to articulate.

"The resemblance is..." Angel muttered, almost at a loss for words.

"She must have been a queen, a high priestess, or perhaps a goddess. Look at this..." I aimed the torch at the mummy's hands—they were clutching an object to its chest.

"It's a book, encased in metal," I observed.

"It's the manuscript," Angel almost babbled, awestruck.

I tried to release the book from the mummy's grasp, but it wouldn't budge. Then I realised that the task wasn't meant for me and stepped back, inviting Angel to take over. She extended a trembling hand toward the book but was startled when the withered, skeletal fingers holding it moved. We both comprehended that the mummy had released the book for her. Suddenly, overcome by dizziness, Angel clutched her forehead and began to sway. As I caught her in my arms, I experienced a blinding flash in my mind's eye ... when it cleared, I found myself in the midst of a fierce battle between native warriors armed with savage weapons. Their bodies bore intricate Celtic-like tattoos, and they clashed with a more advanced group of natives who were dressed and armed like Egyptians.

The air resounded with the cries of the fallen. The battleground was illuminated by burning torches. The leader of the Egyptian faction, Otago, rallied his men against the wild natives. The battlefield was situated in a marsh, a swamp ... they fought ankle-deep in bloodied water, surrounded by the aimlessly floating bodies of the dead.

The Egyptians were losing. Suddenly, a female warrior emerged, adorned with long black hair and clothed in Amazonian-style battle attire. Her nearly naked body was smeared with the blood of her adversaries as she fought her way toward Otago. It was Angel ... she swung a spiked club into the chest of a warrior who was about to strike Otago down. With his blood-soaked, matted hair, Otago acknowledged her kill and called her Asina. They fought together with the intensity of natural-born killers.

Asina cried out triumphantly, her weapon raised high above her head, "Viva! Otago!!... Behind you!!"

Otago swiftly turned and dispatched another attacker. Amidst the chaos, the leader of the opposing force, clad in blood-streaked armour and wielding a long sword, cut through Otago's warriors. He was not of the same race as his men; intuitively, I knew he hailed from Mu. Beside him stood a priest, also a renegade of Mu, holding a pole with a religious icon affixed to its tip. I sensed that these were the forces of darkness, while Otago and Asina represented the forces of good.

The priest clutched the manuscript beneath his arm, and it was clear that the manuscript was the object of their conflict. I heard Vian, the leader of the dark faction say to the priest, "Whatever happens, the manuscript must not fall into the enemy's hands. Take it—bury it! It must remain Mu's property."

Asina saw the priest making a break for it and gave chase. She pursued him and struck him with a powerful blow from her club. She retrieved the book from his grasp and raised it triumphantly into the air.

I watched as Vian charged toward her, sword raised to deliver the final blow. Otago could only watch helplessly ... and he cried out, "Asina, no!"

Vian impaled Asina on his long sword, thrusting it through her until it protruded from her chest. With her dying breath, she cried out, "Otago!"

Vian stood over his victim and declared, "You are no longer the high priestess, Asina!"

Otago raced through the bloody water, driven by desperation to reach Asina.

The priest who had been clubbed regained his footing in the water, his body drenched in blood, madness gleaming in his eyes. He raised the religious icon high above his head, cursing his assailant.

Dying, Asina clung to the manuscript with all her failing strength. A strange storm cloud materialised overhead out of nowhere, crackling with fierce green electric lightning. Thunder roared, resonating through the air. The evening sky darkened suddenly.

All the warriors ceased their battle and gazed in terror at the supernatural storm above them. A bolt of blue lightning arced from the rolling purple storm cloud, striking the book in Asina's grasp. Upon impact, it forked, and one branch of lightning struck the religious icon held aloft by the dying Priest.

Writhing from the electrocution, the priest screamed, "In the name of the Almighty, be cursed for all time to guard the book of death in life."

Otago reached Vian and managed to seize him by the hair, delivering a final, fatal blow by decapitating him.

Asina, now on her knees propped up by Vian's long sword, remained alive, clutching the manuscript to her chest. Otago drove his weapon into the ground and embraced her. Asina died in Otago's powerful arms, yet the manuscript remained firmly gripped in her lifeless hands.

The supernatural storm abruptly dissipated, replaced by a torrential downpour. Otago gazed upward, the heavy rain washing the blood from his face and hair, as he cried out to the gods, "High priestess Asina has been taken ... We are fated to die..."

The warriors let out a collective mournful cry at her passing.

I snapped back to reality, finding myself seated on the floor with Angel in my arms, mirroring Otago's embrace of Asina in her final moments.

"Angel? Angel, come back ... it's Axis." Her eyes fluttered open, and she regained consciousness. Upon realising she was in my arms, still holding the manuscript, she withdrew from me.

"I... I was dreaming ... connected to the manuscript," she

murmured, her voice trembling. "A battle, a past life ... I saw her life, I saw her death."

"Asina?" I asked.

"Yes, you know her name? How?"

"I blacked out after catching you when you collapsed and had the same vision ... Otago, the priest, Vian, the manuscript ... the storm ... right?"

"Yes, but how?"

"We need to close the casket and get out of here, right now."

~ ~ ~

Rita lounged on a beach towel, soaking up the sun at Lindos Beach when a shadow eclipsed her. She lowered her sunglasses, squinting up at the figure blocking the sun.

"Hello, I'm Carmen ... What a day ... This place is magical, isn't it?" Carmen introduced herself.

Rita lowered her sunglasses, assessing Carmen. "Yeah, if you're into doing nothing, honey. Thank God we'll be heading back to civilization in a couple of days. Pull up some sand, kid."

Wearing sunglasses, Carmen spread out her beach towel, slipped off her silk robe, revealing a shapely body in a string bikini—a surprise to Rita, who hadn't expected this from the seemingly slender Chinese girl. Carmen kicked off her towelling slippers and settled down to bask in the sun.

"I bet everyone says that but ends up staying longer," Carmen commented.

Rita poured some coconut oil onto her palm and massaged it into her already tanned, shapely legs. Despite her years, Rita cut a surprisingly youthful figure in her bright red bikini. "Not us ... no, no, once his majesty has spoken ... he'll have his business wrapped up by then, and we'll be out of here."

"Business? Ah, so you're not here on vacation then? ... What kind of business does your husband do?" Carmen inquired.

"He's not my husband, honey. He's in the money game. You

know, make some, lose some, spend as little as possible on anyone but himself."

Carmen chuckled but was slightly taken aback when Rita turned on her side, reached over, and began applying oil to her legs. With her closer, she noticed a bruise on Rita's cheek, obscured until now by her sunglasses.

"Did you have an accident?" Carmen asked, concerned.

"Yeah, walked into a fist. That's what you get for having an intolerant pig for a boyfriend."

"I really enjoyed your singing the other night," Carmen said, attempting to change the subject.

"Turn over, and I'll do your back. It used to be my livelihood, you know, but it's been a while."

Carmen turned over and undid her bikini top for Rita to oil up her back. "You know my boyfriend is an actor. From a famous family … old money."

Rita tapped her on the shoulder; she had finished. Carmen turned over. "Not too bad with the Bruce Lee stuff as well, so I heard."

Rita poured more oil on unsuspecting Carmen, lifted her top, and began gently massaging the oil into her breasts. Carmen was a little rattled by it at first, but then let her continue.

"Charlie is talking about buying this place. You could really turn it into something brilliant, don't you think?"

"He hasn't got a hope, honey. The old boy won't sell. Great job with the breasts, where did you get them done in L.A.? There you go, finished."

"Thank you. They were a gift from my parents in Hong Kong. I had the choice between a car and these."

"You'll get more mileage out of them; you made the right choice, honey," Rita said, laying back down.

"Mr Harris has already told Charlie he'll sell to him on the proviso he preserves the jungle, as a caveat. He'll only sell to someone he can trust, Charlie said."

"Well, take it from me, sister. Tell your Charlie boy to save his breath. Vinny and his mob have the plans for redevelopment already underway. The bulldozers are waiting in the wings."

Carmen sat up and retied her top. "Really ... Mr Harris doesn't seem the type to double-deal."

"Not everything is as it seems, Carmen. Take that from a true survivor. Harris has no say in it. One way or the other, Vinny and his thugs will get it. I've seen them do it before. Vinny makes a Goddamned living out of getting what he wants and gets it any way he can. I'm living testimony to that."

"Well, if that's so, then I hope they leave the forest the way it is."

"Ha! You've gotta be kidding, honey. That's what it's all about. The timber is worth squillions."

"Roland won't sell to them if they're going to turn it into chopsticks?"

"They'll pulp the crap out of it," Rita confided.

"Do you love him?" Carmen probed a little deeper.

"Vinny? Look, some people mimic love; to them, it's only a confection." She got to her feet, removed her glasses revealing a shiner. "This black eye is a result of confection. You don't get one from love. I'm going to take a swim. Just warn your Charlie boy, Vinny and his henchmen aren't the sort to mess with; they don't tolerate competition." She held out a hand to Carmen, who took it, and together they walked the short distance to the turquoise water.

CHAPTER
NINE

I looked up at the rope swinging ten feet above us. "Give me your foot," I told Angel, cupping my hands to take it.

"Then how are you going to get out?"

She locked her foot into my grip, and I lifted her up.

"Stand on my shoulders," I said, straining.

She took one last forlorn look at Richard's corpse, climbed up onto my shoulders, reached for the rope, got it, and then hauled herself up. No sooner was she out of the hole than I emerged.

Amazed, she exclaimed, "How on earth did you manage that?"

"A trick I learned from an old Indian," I said, puffing.

As we were making our way out of the temple, the meaning of what I'd said dawned on her.

She stopped and giggled. "I just got it, you learned it from an old Indian ... the Indian rope trick ... sure. You!" She playfully thumped me in the bicep. I grabbed her arm, pulled her close, and kissed her.

~ ~ ~

Dino shut down my laptop, slipped out of our room, ensured the corridor was clear, then stealthily entered Vitale's room.

Vinny looked up from his armchair, puffing on a cigar. "So, who is this Axis Stone, and what's he doing here?"

"My guess is he's a treasure hunter," Dino replied.

"Him and how many other half-assed foreign gold-diggers," Vitale quipped through a haze of cigar smoke.

"Nah, I don't think he's a gold digger. Judging by his notes, he knows his stuff."

Vinny stood up, draped an arm around the slightly taller man's shoulders, and escorted him to the door. "And how would you fucking know that, Dino?"

"Both you and the boss told me to investigate him, so I did. You got an issue with that?"

"No, I don't," Vitale said, removing his arm to let Dino depart. "Hey, where are you from?"

"Me? Just like you … Italiano, Americano … I call myself a pizza; the best of everything sitting on top of a lump of dough."

They shared a chuckle.

~ ~ ~

Tong's hands skilfully assembled the stock and barrel of a collapsible .222 calibre sniper's rifle. He then affixed a silencer to the barrel before placing the rifle by the open window in his room. He rested his elbows on the windowsill and took aim.

Roland was hobbling along the jetty toward the Lindos Lady. A red laser dot suddenly appeared on his back and then tracked up to the back of his head.

Tong's finger caressed the trigger.

Just as he prepared to fire, Charlie emerged from the workshed on the pier, inadvertently shielding Roland from Tong's aim. The laser dot now rested on the back of Charlie's head.

Bang! The jeep backfired as I shifted gears, pushing the old vehicle to its limits on the bumpy dirt road back to Hotel Lindos.

Angel exclaimed, "I can't believe all of this is happening. Talk about coincidences. In just a few hours, we found something that poor Richard had been searching after for years. It's as if he led us right to it. And then that mummy's face, the vision, the manuscript ... Holy-heck, what does it all mean?"

"We might get a better idea once I can decipher the text."

"Can you do that? I thought you were a—"

"I'll use some software I know of..."

"Look at that," she shouted.

"What?" I replied, glancing around while struggling with the steering wheel.

"Out at sea ... That's one serious hurricane heading our way." She grabbed the two-way handset from the dashboard.

~ ~ ~

Back at the hotel, Boy was on the two-way. "Angel, we've received a warning from the Met. It's a category five hurricane, with winds of 157 miles per hour or more. A really bad one. The Met called it catastrophic. See you soon. Over." He then called out, "Cora! Cora! Close all the shutters; a big hurricane is coming. We need to bring all the guests to the bar."

Roland hobbled into the lobby with Charlie and said, "Boy, there's a severe hurricane rapidly approaching from the east. You'll need to..."

"Yes, sir. Angel called on the two-way. I'm to get the shutters down and assemble the guests and staff in the bar."

"Good, good. Where is she?"

"On her way here, sir. She will attend to Lindos Lady. The Met estimates it's still three hours away from making landfall."

"I estimate it to be about three hours before it hits us."

Charlie and Boy exchanged amused glances as Roland essentially repeated what Boy had already told him.

"Need a hand?" Charlie offered Boy.

"Yes, could you please fetch Miss Carmen and Miss Rita? They went to the beach."

Roland looked earnestly at Charlie and instructed urgently, "Go, son ... go!"

Charlie hurried out through the front doors.

"I'll be in my study, Boy. I expect you'll be relocating the guests to the bar?"

"Good idea, boss," Boy said, playing along to humour the old man.

As Roland hobbled toward his study, he mumbled aloud to himself, "It's going to be a bad one. I can feel the depression in the air, my bones are aching ... Everyone will start acting strangely soon ... it's the magnetism, you know ... the madness is caused by fear and magnetism."

~ ~ ~

Charlie jogged along the path to the beach. The breeze had intensified, gusting forcefully and making it challenging for him to run in a straight line. The palm trees swayed, sending a warning of their own.

~ ~ ~

A few hours later, I sat at the desk in my room, trying to decipher the manuscript. I had been using AI, but the impending hurricane had severed the satellite internet connection. Luckily, I had decoded enough to continue without it. There might be no cellphone signal here but at least the dish on the roof gave us the internet, except in a storm. I took a sip of JD and leaned back in my chair, frustrated. It felt like another dead end. In annoyance, I tore a page from my notepad, crumpled it into a ball, and tossed it over my shoulder in the direction of the wastepaper basket near the door. It missed and joined the growing collection of failed shots scattered on the floor.

A forceful knock on the door interrupted my thoughts, and I called out, "Who's there?"

"Charlie Chan, can I have a word?"

"Man, I'm really busy. Can it wait?"

"No."

"Okay, come in, it's open."

Charlie entered and immediately noticed the mess of crumpled paper balls strewn across the floor. He couldn't help but smile wryly. "Sorry to disturb you, but we really need to talk."

I leaned back in my chair, chewing on the end of my ballpoint pen. "Sit down Charlie ... What's the drama?"

Charlie complied. "I want to be honest with you ... I was invited here by Mr Harris to solve his problems. I need to know what you've discovered. Trust me, I wouldn't ask if it weren't a matter of life and death."

"You and me both," I responded.

"Meaning?"

"I was invited here by Roland for the same reason."

"Yes, well, my brief is more about keeping both Mr Harris and Angel safe."

There was another knock at the door. Before I could speak, Charlie said, "That'll be Carmen. Come in!" he called out.

"Wait, I'm not into a social—" I started to complain.

Carmen came in and took a seat. "I was just telling Mr Stone about our brief ... He also has a brief, but his was to look into Richard's disappearance while ours is to keep the Harris family safe."

"I think both things are connected," she admitted.

"You're talking about our excursion to the ruin today ... Okay, I'm into saving lives too ... But it's a long story ... and a pretty weird one ... pretty tough for a guy such as yourself to handle."

I didn't miss the two of them exchanging a shrewd glance. Charlie fired me a wry smile, "Try me."

The wind outside had escalated to gale force, causing the old timber hotel to shudder with every gust.

As waves crashed over the bow of the Lindos Lady, and the cruiser was violently tossed against the mooring, Angel found herself in a formidable battle to secure the vessel against the approaching tempest.

Vitale, Rita, and Raman were seated at the bar, with Boy tending to them. Tong and Dino occupied a nearby table. Vitale, fuelled by alcohol, was becoming increasingly obnoxious.

Raman, growing frustrated, had decided to return to the city before nightfall. "This damned storm could leave me stranded here."

"I don't like it at all," grumbled Rita. "A hurricane of this size could reduce this rickety old dump to matchsticks in an instant. We wouldn't stand a chance."

"You mightn't need your bulldozers after all," Vitale chuckled. "Here, Raman, have another drink ... it's on this rickety old dump." He topped up Raman's glass, and Rita extended hers for a refill as well. She was already quite intoxicated, and the impending hurricane had pushed their nerves to the edge.

"Rita will take a refill too ... sweetie pie."

"No she won't," Vitale snapped. "Rita's had her fill ... Tong, Dino, come over here and drink with us."

"Getting shit-faced won't get rid of the hurricane, Vitale," Dino responded.

"What's your problem pal. Chicken-shit scared of a lousy storm?" Vitale taunted Dino, causing him to jump up, ready to fight. But Tong quickly intervened, grabbing Dino by the arm and pulling him back into his chair.

"We'll see who's chicken-shit. If a Tsunami the size of a 747 hits this joint ... Ha! Then we'll see who's chicken shit!" Dino exclaimed.

Vitale's anxiety was palpable as the impending doom weighed on him. He downed his drink and snapped, "Enough of this! Let's hop in the limo and get out of Dodge before this damn storm has a chance to harm any of us."

"Sure, Vinny. Got any more brilliant ideas?" Rita spat. "I think I'd rather be here than swept out to sea in a limo."

Vinny's agitation continued to escalate. Raman intervened, "Let's put an end to this hostility. Don't you know that the magnetic effects of a storm can make people act irrationally? You're all thinking strangely. Now, let's just calm down."

Vitale, unable to stay still, began pacing around. "Yeah, yeah, let's forget all this doom and gloom crap ... everything will turn out roses, won't it, Raman?"

A powerful gust of wind rattled the hotel's walls, halting Vitale's pacing.

"Look at it this way, Vinny," Raman whispered, waving Vitale closer with a sly smile. "The storm might be an advantage. An accident involving the old man, perhaps?" A smug expression crossed Vitale's rugged face as Raman continued in a hushed tone, "You see, a little bit of logic, and the storm will take the blame."

~ ~ ~

Charlie was impressed by my account of the Lost City, the discovery of Richard's body, and what I had deciphered from the manuscript thus far.

"Absolutely awesome," he declared.

"So who do you think built the city? ... Who were the people?" Carmen asked eagerly.

"Good questions. The ruin looked ancient, maybe it even predates the Maya or the Olmecs."

Carmen was getting right into it, "What about the manuscript, who wrote that?"

"Until more can be deciphered, I can't tell. I'm just a humble PI, no expert; what we need is a qualified archaeologist."

Charlie asked, "In your opinion, was Richard murdered?"

"Going by the hole in the back of his skull, I'd have to say yes. I've got a theory."

Charlie sat back in his chair, "Okay, let's hear it."

"Someone with an eye on the area found out that Richard had discovered the ruin, and they wanted it hushed up."

"But why?" Carmen questioned.

Charlie was nodding his head, "Interesting hypothesis ... very interesting."

~ ~ ~

Roland and Angel came out of the study and stopped in the lobby. Lightning flashed, thunder sounded.

"I'd like you to get Richard's remains as soon as possible ... we need to give him a proper burial," Roland said remorsefully.

"Don't worry, Pop," she said, concerned for the old man. "As soon as the hurricane has passed and we've cleaned up the mess, I'll go and get him. Are you all right?"

He propped himself up against the front desk, holding his chest, breathing erratically while flexing his right arm. Worried, Angel looked him over. His face was pale, his hands were trembling. He nodded he was okay, went to move but she stopped him.

"No, not so fast, feller ... You haven't convinced me you're all right ... Just chill for a minute; it's been a lot to take on board."

"I'm fine, my dear. It's just confirmation after all this time that my boy is dead," he paused as a tear trickled down his cheek. "It makes the old heart weigh heavy with sorrow."

She embraced him for a tender moment, and they both wept. During the embrace, a vision flashed in Angel's mind of legs crumbling, a walking stick falling in slow motion, the sound of it striking the ground repeating and echoing.

"I'm here with you, Pop," she said tenderly, sobbing.

"I know, Lassie ... I know ... Give me a hand to the barroom where we'll be safe."

She produced an oily cloth from the back pocket of her dungarees and dabbed his eyes dry, then her own.

"You've been wiping the engine with that cloth," he chuckled. A commotion erupted from the barroom attracting their attention. "It's that damned fool Vitale giving Boy a hard time again," Roland growled.

He tried to move towards the barroom, but Angel held his arm.

"No, Pop, don't ... you're too upset. Leave it to me."

"Damned if I will," he snarled.

CHAPTER
TEN

Roland shuffled into the barroom, his face flushed with anger. He found Vitale gripping Boy's lapels, glaring at him. The rest of Vitale's gang, except for the inebriated Rita slumped on a barstool, were seated at a nearby table, watching the scene with amusement.

"Listen, you freaking rodent," Vitale snarled inches from Boy's terrified face. "When I order a drink, I expect it to get one with booze in it. The service in this joint is crap." He emptied what remained in his glass over Boy's head.

"Release Boy, Vitale," Roland bellowed, his voice dripping with venom. "You and your despicable associates, get out of my hotel. I won't tolerate vermin like you treating my staff like slaves."

Vitale's eyes were fixed manically on Roland, who was visibly struggling to maintain his composure.

Raman chimed in nonchalantly, "Why not, Mr Harris? They're essentially your indentured servants, aren't they? They've been slaves to foreigners ever since the Spanish conquest. The storm is approaching, Vinny."

This was the signal Vitale had been waiting for, and he released his grip on Boy.

"I know who you are and what you represent, Raman. I won't engage in a battle of wits with an unarmed man."

"Yes, Major Harris ... generous of you to share some of your antiquated wisdom with us. We'll just waltz out into the hurricane and be gone, shall we?" Vitale taunted sarcastically.

"You deserve nothing less, Vitale. Your kind is nothing but trash."

Vitale pretended to brush non-existent lint from Boy's white jacket and then punched him in the stomach. Boy doubled over, gasping for breath. Roland's patience wore thin, and he staggered towards Vitale, swinging one of his walking sticks menacingly.

"If I were ten years younger, I'd deal with you. Get out of here, you lout, before I summon the police!"

Vitale easily deflected Roland's feeble attempt with his stick. Angel intervened, restraining Roland.

Vitale confronted Roland with a menacing snarl, "You're just a half-dead, old fart. Get out of my freakin' face."

Angel couldn't take it any longer, "Enough, Vitale! I'm calling the police!"

Raman nonchalantly commented, "That won't be necessary, Mrs Harris. The police are already here. Please relay your complaint to Officer Rosario."

Dino, leaning back in his chair, displayed his badge with a smug look and said, "Is there a problem, Mrs Harris?"

Unable to bear any more, Roland, wielding his cane like a sword, shrieked, "Damn hoodlums!" and launched another attack on Vitale, this time with more intensity. His cane was raised high, ready to strike, but in a sudden flash of lightning and a deafening clap of thunder, Roland froze. The cane slipped from his grasp, his knees buckled, and Angel watched in horror as her vision became a chilling reality. Gasping, Roland collapsed, and the cane bounced slowly on the floor, its sound echoing eerily.

Rita jolted upright with a gasp of dread.

Vitale found the situation entertaining, just as Raman had suggested, "Well, well, look at that, the Major is having a heart attack."

Raman had a smug grin as he silently praised Vitale with "Well done."

Angel dropped to her knees beside Roland, taking his hand and sobbing. She searched for a pulse but was met with the horrifying realisation that there was none.

"Oh no! Pop ... no!" she screamed.

She looked up at Vinny, standing menacingly over her, and seized one of Roland's walking sticks. She got to her feet and swung it forcefully at Vitale, hitting him hard on the shoulder. The blow stung more from the assault on his pride. Vitale drew his pistol, grimacing from the pain in his shoulder, and aimed it at Angel. She froze, the stick poised for another strike, but decided against it and lowered it.

Vitale delivered a brutal backhand slap across Angel's face, but she bravely stood her ground. Boy rushed to her side.

"You're a tough one, aren't you?" Vitale sneered.

"You piece of shit!" Angel shouted. Boy had to restrain her. "There are witnesses—"

Before she could finish her sentence, Vitale lunged, grabbed her by the hair, and pressed the barrel of his .38 against her cheek.

"Let her go, Vinny!" Rita yelled with bitterness.

Raman signalled to Rita to refrain from provoking Vitale further. Dino got up from the table, walked over to Roland on the floor, glanced down at him, and casually remarked, "Natural causes. What a pity."

Vitale let go of Angel. His shoulder still ached from the earlier blow, and he winced in pain.

An unexpected loud bang made everyone flinch. It was the approaching hurricane's reminder, as debris struck the hotel's exterior. Lightning illuminated the room, followed by a deafening clap of thunder. Outside, the dark thunderheads had turned day into night. The house lights flickered, and tension in the room escalated.

Though Angel was distraught, she managed to maintain her composure and instructed Boy to request Cora to bring hurricane lamps.

Vitale pointed his gun at her, beads of perspiration forming on his forehead, and ordered, "I give the orders here! What lamps?"

Boy halted on his way to Cora and calmly informed Vitale, "The lights will soon go out, Mr Vitale; we need hurricane lamps."

Waving the gun nonchalantly, Vitale grumbled, "Fine, fine, do it. Tong, keep an eye on him. Dino, go upstairs and bring the others down. If they resist, shoot them."

Dino sought confirmation from Raman, annoyed by Vitale's orders. Raman nodded his approval.

"Raman, assist me with Harris. And you," Vitale pointed his gun at Angel, "sit over there with Rita. If I hear a single word from you, Boy and Cora get wasted. Understood?"

Angel complied and settled on a barstool. Rita offered her a consoling embrace.

Vitale poured himself another JD and downed it.

The telephone rang, and Angel made a move to answer it, but Rita restrained her.

Vitale left Raman to attend to Roland's body and took the call himself.

"Hello. Yes, this is the Hotel ... What?... Hello! Hello!" He slammed the phone down in anger. "The line is down! What next?"

Rita checked her cellphone. "There's no signal."

Vitale berated her, "Are you dense? Of course, there's no freakin' signal. Haven't you noticed the storm outside?"

The lights went out, plunging the room into darkness. I fumbled to find my torch and switched it on. The three of us prepared to descend the stairs when Dino burst into the room.

I directed the torch at him, and he reacted, "Get that out of my eyes. Mr Harris wants all of you in the barroom. It's too dangerous up here."

The room groaned audibly as the wind battered it.

"No problem, we'll be there in a couple of minutes. I need to retrieve something from my room first," Charlie responded.

Lightning flashed, and thunder rumbled. In the brief illumination, I noticed that Dino had drawn a pistol and was aiming it at Charlie.

"Why the gun?" I inquired.

"Mind your business, now move."

We reluctantly filed out.

Carmen led the way, followed by me, and Charlie with Dino closely behind.

Charlie suddenly stopped part way down the stairs. In the darkness, Dino bumped into him. Swift as lightning, Charlie reached down between his legs, grabbed Dino's leg, and pulled. Dino tumbled backward, his head thudding against the step, and the pistol discharged simultaneously with a lightning flash and a deafening clap of thunder.

Realising that the gunshot might have been masked by the thunderclap, I quickly guided Carmen to take cover behind the front desk. Charlie retrieved the pistol from the unconscious Dino.

Vitale abruptly ceased his pacing, his head jerking up as if uncertain whether he had heard a gunshot or merely thunder. His nerves were frayed, beads of sweat glistening on his face, and his trembling hand clutched the gun. Cora, methodically placing hurricane lamps around the room, cast eerie shadows on the walls and ceiling with their dim light. Boy was stationed behind the bar, while Tong sat beside Raman.

"That wasn't thunder, it was a shot," Vitale said nervously.

"No, it was just thunder, Vinny. Why don't you sit down and relax? You're making me nervous with all that pacing, like a cat on a hot tin roof," Raman remarked.

A flash of lightning followed by a deafening thunderclap filled the room. Vitale brandished his pistol, waving it around. "Relax, you say ... well, I'm telling you, it was a damn gunshot!"

He went to the lobby door, positioning himself defensively, and called out anxiously, "Dino? Dino? Are you there? .... Answer me!" The heavy rain had started pounding on the windows and the corrugated iron roof.

Vitale couldn't fathom why Dino hadn't responded. He turned to

Raman and Tong, his eyes filled with panic. "It's Chan, I'm telling you ... If he's got Dino, he's got his gun."

At that moment, I entered the room. As soon as I saw the gun in Vitale's hand, I stopped in my tracks. A quick glance at Angel revealed her distress.

Vitale swung the gun in my direction. "You! Jones! Get in here! Where are the others? Dino?" he demanded.

I raised my hands halfway, maintaining my composure. "Jones?" I responded with a light-hearted tone to avoid agitating him. "Hey, Vinny, take it easy. You look a bit jumpy. They're upstairs playing chess ... Dino's keeping an eye on them. What's with the piece? Is something wrong?"

Lightning illuminated the room, thunder rattled the hotel, and the deafening rainstorm outside made it challenging to hear, let alone think straight.

"He killed Pop!" Angel screamed.

"What?" I shouted.

Vitale nodded at Tong, who rose from his chair like a giant, grabbed me, carried me across the room, and deposited me on a barstool next to Angel.

"Thanks, Tong. If you had asked, I could have made it here on my own," I quipped, glancing at Angel. "What happened?"

"Shut up!" Vitale yelled frantically. "Not another word from any of you, or you'll join the old man on the floor. Tong, use Cora as cover and go check on Dino. I don't trust this guy. At the first sign of trouble, waste her."

Tong drew his pistol, seized Cora by her long black hair, and pushed her toward the lobby.

"I don't understand all the commotion. Why are you terrorizing these people, Vinny? None of us are likely to make it anyway..."

"I said shut up! What do you mean we're not going to make it?"

"The eye of the storm is about to hit us. While I was upstairs, I heard parts of the roof being torn off. I'd estimate we have about ten minutes before this place collapses like a house of cards."

Lightning flashed again, followed by a sharp clap of thunder.

"Notice how quickly the thunder follows the lightning? After a flash, you count: one thousand and one, one thousand and two, one thousand and three ... each thousand is a second, and each second is a mile before the hurricane strikes. By my reckoning, it's about two miles away."

Angel chimed in, "Pop said the place couldn't withstand another hit. The last major hurricane was five years ago, and it nearly obliterated us ... and that was nothing compared to this one."

Angel had grasped my intention: I was deliberately trying to further unravel Vitale.

I gestured towards the old chandelier above our heads, which was swinging back and forth. It was clear that it was getting to Vitale. He nervously paced up and down; the storm was clearly getting under his skin. He abruptly halted, wiping his sweat-drenched brow, and muttered, "Alright, alright, when the others get down, we're getting out of here."

"Come on, Vinny, be realistic. Where would we go?" Raman chimed in. "Don't pay attention to them; they're just trying to mess with your head."

"I don't give a damn, it's giving me the creeps, you hear? The creeps."

Suddenly, an enormous crash resounded as a tree branch smashed through the window, accompanied by a powerful gust of wind and torrential rain. Vitale panicked.

I shouted at him, "That's the thing about nature, Vinny ... it's in control, not you. Doesn't sit well with you, does it?"

"Shut up, you jerk. What makes you so tough, huh? I'll show you tough." He aimed the gun at me. "Get over there and close that damn window!"

I discreetly uncocked the .38 I had been holding, which originally belonged to Dino. There was a maelstrom inside the room, every that wasn't tied down flying about like a mini tornado. Ramon and Boy had swiftly jumped up, pulling the branch inside and forcing the shutters closed. Even though calm now prevailed with the storm shut out, Rita sensed the tension had gone up a notch, and tried to distract Vitale.

"I think we all could use a drink," she suggested.

"Yeah, a drink. That's what I need," Vitale agreed. "Boy, fetch me a bottle, or I'll blow your face off."

I quietly uncocked the .38, relieved to see a temporary distraction taking place.

CHAPTER
ELEVEN

Tong pushed Cora ahead of him to the base of the stairs, halting her there. He scanned the surroundings for any signs of trouble. Carmen emerged from the darkness and confronted them. Upon seeing that Tong was holding a gun, she quickly raised her hands.

"Hey, mister, I'm unarmed, see ... If you're looking for your friend, he's upstairs with Charlie. They'll be down in a minute," Carmen said, trying to distract Tong long enough for Charlie to make his move. And Charlie did just that. He jumped out from behind the staircase and snatched the pistol out of Tong's hand. Carmen seized the opportunity to pull Cora away. Charlie aimed the gun at Tong and ordered, "Back up against the railing. I will shoot if you disobey." Tong complied, and Charlie proceeded to fasten Tong's wrists together around the banister, then gagged him. Lightning flashed, followed almost immediately by thunder; the hurricane was right on top of them, and it was loud.

I watched impatiently as Vitale paced the floor, his nervous energy making me uneasy. Carmen entered, followed closely by Charlie. Vitale swung around, aiming his gun at them. They stopped abruptly and raised their hands. Charlie shot me a sly wink.

"That's far enough, Chan ... where's Dino and Tong?" Vitale demanded.

"Right behind us," Charlie said with a convincing look of surprise on his face. "What's this all about?"

"Drop your piece, Vitale," I said clearly, aiming the .38 at him. Vitale pivoted to face me, and Charlie pressed his pistol into the back of Vitale's head.

"Don't want to lose your head, Vitale ... I'll take that," Charlie said, snatching the pistol out of Vitale's hand.

"Smart, real smart ... You'll be sorry you did this, Chinaman." Charlie pushed his pistol hard into Vitale's back to silence him.

I aimed at Raman and ordered, "Put your gun on the table, Raman."

"I don't carry a gun; it's far too vulgar," he said calmly.

"Sit down, Vitale," Charlie commanded. When Vitale hesitated, he pushed the gun into his chest to force him into the chair.

Vitale's eyes narrowed, "I warned you before ... be careful who you're pushing around, sonny."

"Carmen, could you get Cora, please?" Charlie said, ignoring Vitale.

Lightning flashed, and after a few seconds, thunder resounded; it was a little more distant. The lights flickered back on.

"It's passing," Angel said.

"Look, I know you people are bothered by some things, but you're not professionals ... You don't wave guns around convincingly ... It doesn't look safe ... you know what I'm..."

I cut Raman off. "Oh, shut the fuck up, or I'll shove this thing up your rear end and blow your brains out."

Carmen entered with Cora.

"That's all of us except for Tong and Dino ... where's Mr Harris?" Charlie asked Angel.

"Vitale killed him," she said, tears welling up in her eyes.

"He suffered a coronary," I corrected.

"I'm sorry, Mrs Harris. He was a very special man and a dear family friend. He will be greatly missed."

"We're all in tears," Vitale said facetiously. "Now what's all this about? Who the hell are you? You're no actor, that's for sure, and you're no Indiana Jones."

"I'm a private detective and an actor," Charlie said.

"Oh, how funny ... Charlie Chan, PI," Vitale chuckled.

"I'd be careful who I was threatening if I were you, Vitale. I'm also a private detective," I said.

Raman was shaking his head, highly amused, "We're surrounded by private eyes. Who the hell hired two of you?"

"And for what?" Vitale added.

"The Major retained both of us, me to safeguard the family, and Axis to locate his son's body," Charlie said.

Angel looked surprised.

"I know, Mrs Harris. I'm sorry you weren't told, but the major had his reasons," Charlie explained. "His primary concern was for your safety. Richard had disappeared under dubious circumstances. The major believed he was murdered. Mr Raman, do you know anything about an ancient ruin on this property?"

Raman held open his hands piously, palms up. "Everyone knows about it. It's of no cultural significance."

"What's all this got to do with anything?" Vitale barked.

I'd had enough of him. "Why don't you just shut up and listen."

"Ha! That'd be a first," Rita mumbled. Vitale gave her an evil glare.

"So, you do know about the ruin? Then who tried to destroy it and why?" Charlie questioned.

"That's ancient history, years ago. A mill owner who was contesting Harris's title to the property. He thought the government would stop his takeover bid if they knew about the ruin. His name was Ong, I think. You'd remember him, Mrs Harris?"

"Yes, I remember Pop mentioning his name. Pop won the case. That was six years ago," Angel said.

"Correct. Now, would our Mr Ong have wanted Richard out of the way?" Raman asked.

Angel suddenly looked uncomfortable. "Mr Chan, Axis and I found Richard's body today. I don't think any of this is necessary.

Pop's dead. What's done is done, for God's sake."

"Not quite, Mrs Harris. Please indulge me, I must continue ... for the Major's sake, you understand?"

Angel tried to appeal, but I placated her. "Go on, Charlie," I said.

"We can safely assume that you, Mr Raman, had nothing to do with Richard's death. You and Vitale are only guilty of conspiracy to commit the murder of Roland and Angel Harris."

"Ha! I'd like to see you make that stick, Chan!" Vitale said.

"That could prove to be a very damaging accusation, Mr Chan. Like Mr Vitale intimated, you'd better have proof," Raman said coldly.

"No problem, Mr Raman, all of your conversations at this Hotel have been recorded ... but more on that later. First, I must present my theory as to who killed Richard Harris. Apart from myself, one other person in this room has suspected who the murderer was, and she has kept it her secret since then, haven't you, Mrs Harris?"

Angel's expression soured.

"Wait a minute, Charlie, I think you might be going a tad too far," I said.

"Hear me out, Axis. You couldn't say anything to Roland, could you, Angel?"

Angel glanced at me with uncertainty and then back at Charlie.

"It was Mike! He was insanely jealous. He could have gone there that day ... He knew Richard was at the dig, I'd told him ... How did you find out about him?" Angel asked, then looked at me as though I'd betrayed her trust. "You promised," she muttered to me.

Charlie was pacing the floor like an Agatha Christie detective in a room full of butlers.

"Axis told me nothing. I checked on you. You arrived at Lindos Hotel on September 1st, 2013. In 2012, you had registered a complaint with the police of rape by one Mike Mendoza. Later, you dropped the charge. Correct?"

Angel was tearing up. She nodded. "He threatened to kill me."

Before he was released from remand, you came here. I checked car hire and bus records and found that Mike Mendoza arrived at the Hotel Lindos on September 12th, 2013, on the early bus."

I was impressed by Charlie's investigative skills.

"What are you suggesting, Mr Chan?" Angel asked.

I took her hand. "Relax, Angel."

"It's all right, Mrs Harris. I am not accusing you of anything. Mr Mendoza probably fought with Richard, and the fight probably resulted in Richard's death. But that is no longer possible to prove and not really the object of this exercise."

"So what happened to Mendoza?" I asked.

Charlie stopped pacing and faced us with a wry smile on his face. "Oh, he still exists, changed his name to M. J. Ong." We were all shocked. "That's correct … the mill owner, Mr Raman, told us tried to destroy the ruin."

Charlie walked over to Raman. "And if my information is correct, Mr M. J. Ong is a major shareholder in R.O. Developments, which is one of your companies, is it not, Mr Raman? I can safely state that the mysterious Mr Ong is, in fact, your partner."

Angel was stunned. "That's unbelievable. Mike Mendoza is Ong?"

Vitale piped up, "So what? For Christ's sake. This is boring as bat crap."

"It means, Mr Raman here won't make it to mayor, and you'll get a stint in jail. Now, that you will find boring," Charlie concluded.

"Interesting conclusion, Chan, but this kangaroo court—"

Charlie interrupted Vitale, "Angel, is it your wish for the forests of Lindos estate to be preserved in perpetuity?"

"Yes," she affirmed, "most definitely."

"And Axis, you told me deforestation is causing soil erosion, which in turn affects water clarity, ultimately endangering the coral reefs … thereby destroying tourism."

"Salinity," Rita posed, staring at Vitale with an 'I told you so' expression.

"Correct," I affirmed.

Charlie continued, "Well, with your permission, Mrs Harris, I think a deal could be structured. Mr Raman, if you become mayor, you could do a lot to ensure the preservation of the natural environment. Now, it is possible that after I document my findings and pass on the brief and tapes to Mrs Harris, she might choose not to make the information public or press charges."

"Yeah, clever move, Chan," Vitale said smugly.

Charlie ignored him. "However, I'm sure she will choose to keep the information in a very safe place for insurance and copy her attorney. Should a breach of this agreement occur, then you will be exposed. Will your partner Mr Ong agree with these terms, Mr Raman?"

"I think you'll find all parties will abide by your proposal," Raman agreed.

"So do we have a deal in principle, Mr Raman?"

"Yes, we have a deal in principle, Mr Chan."

Charlie turned his attention to Angel. "And you, Mrs Harris, do you agree?"

"Yes, I agree in principle."

I walked out onto the porch to assess the storm damage, as much as I could discern in the darkness. Broken window shutters flapped in the breeze. Sheets of corrugated iron that had been ripped from the roof dangled in the giant fronds of the surrounding palm trees.

"It appears Mrs Harris was correct," Charlie's voice emanated from behind me. "The hurricane has passed, and I believe that with its passing came the winds of change. I advised Mr Raman that it would be best for him and his companions to depart."

Just then, Raman, Vitale, and the other two emerged onto the porch on their way to the limousine. They paused, and Raman remarked, "You're proficient at your job, Chan."

"I left one of my toiletry bags in the bathroom. Retrieve it when you return upstairs to collect your belongings. Get Boy to help you," Vitale discourteously snapped at Rita, who had arrived, panting and struggling with Vitale's luggage.

She dropped his bags and snarled, "Fetch it yourself. I won't be needing my luggage; I plan to stay here for a few more days."

"Not on my dime you won't!" Vitale argued.

I approached Rita and gave Vitale a stern look. "No, it's on the house. I told her she can stay as long as she likes."

"Since when do you give orders around here, Stone?" Vitale barked.

I retorted, "Since you lost the fight, Vitale. Now, get out of here before you end up in more trouble."

We faced off in a tense Mexican standoff for a moment, then Vitale glared at Rita and, with malice in his tone, said, "No woman gives me the bullet ... When you come crawling back like you've done plenty of times before, you won't be surprised by the reception."

"Leave, Vitale," Charlie growled. He had lost patience with the man. "There'll be trouble if you return. Do I make myself clear? Oh, and that's not a threat; it's a promise."

Vitale glared at Charlie for a long moment, then turned to Tong. "Put the luggage in the trunk, Tong." He got into the backseat of the limo. The others followed, and Tong took the driver's seat. The four of us watched the limo depart.

Charlie glanced at me, "It was considerate of you to see them off."

"I wasn't here to bid farewell; it was to ensure they departed."

Vitale's arm protruded from the window, displaying a raised middle finger.

"Don't think he likes you, Chan," I commented.

"Don't be ridiculous, my friend; the finger was clearly meant for you."

We watched the black limo merge into the night and then returned inside. "Glad to see the back of them," I stated to Chan.

"Unfortunately, my friend, I don't think it's over yet. As a matter of fact, I believe it has only just begun."

"No, please, anything but 'white lace and promises'," I quipped.

Boy approached us in the lobby. "Mrs Harris requested a meeting in the study. Shall I bring tea, Sir?"

Charlie nodded, and Boy scurried off. "'White lace and

promises'?" he inquired.

I whistled the opening verse of the Carpenters' song as we strolled together toward the study. Charlie chuckled at the gag.

CHAPTER
TWELVE

Dawn was breaking. Angel sat in Roland's chair, gazing at the photographs on the wall. Her distress over losing Roland had now fully settled in. She wiped her eyes and looked at Carmen, saying sadly, "It won't be the same around here without Pop."

"I know. But I think there's still plenty of his spirit here," Carmen replied.

Angel managed a smile through her tears. Charlie and I entered and settled into chairs. I turned to check on Paddy. "All this gangster stuff is tiring, isn't it, Paddy?"

Angel reminded me, "He won't answer you, Axis; he's a dummy."

We all took a moment to look around the room and remember the major.

"I can't begin to thank you for all you've done, Charlie," Angel said, her voice trembling with emotion.

"No problem," Charlie replied.

"Did Pop work out your fee and everything?"

"Let's not worry about that," Charlie reassured her.

"You're welcome to stay with us for as long as you want, on the house, of course. That goes for you too, Axis."

We acknowledged her offer with a smile. We could all sense that Angel was on the brink of an emotional outburst, making the conversation feel awkward.

"How long will it take you to decipher the manuscript, Axis?" Angel inquired.

"I don't know ... As I've said, I'm a PI, only an amateur antiquary, but after I get a little shuteye, I might be able to make more progress, assuming the internet is back."

"It is," Angel confirmed.

I asked, "When do you want to go back to the ruin, Angel?"

Emotion welled up in her again, and she hesitated, "Um ... well... Pop wanted to be buried with Richard..."

Charlie nudged me with his elbow and looked up, suggesting that we should take Angel upstairs. "I think we could all use some rest."

I got up and went to Angel, gently holding her by the shoulders, looking into her eyes, and wiping away her tears. "Come on, kiddo, let's go..."

"Axis, what am I going to do now that Pop's gone?"

I held her close as she cried on my shoulder. The others gave us some privacy.

"How could you let Vitale get away with killing him?" she sobbed.

I held her at arm's length, trying to comfort her, "Hey, come on now ... Roland had a heart attack."

She violently pulled away from me and erupted in a hysterical rage, punching my chest with her fists.

"He didn't! ... He killed him! ... He's a murderer!"

I pulled her close again, understanding her grief. She needed someone to blame for Roland's loss.

"It's all right, love, let it out ... go on..."

"Why did he have to die? I loved him so much."

"I know ... I know..." I said, doing my best to comfort her.

"He was like a father to me ... Now, I've got no-one."

"It's all right, kid... You've got me," I reassured her.

I had barely slept, and by midday, I was still diligently trying to decipher the manuscript, feeling completely out of my depth. Then, something caught my attention. I looked up at the ceiling fan and exclaimed, "Holy mackerel!" I tucked the manuscript under my arm and dashed out of the room.

I found Boy in the lobby and asked, "Where is everyone?" My frenetic demeanour left him speechless. Without waiting for an answer, I headed for the front door.

Boy called after me, "Sir, Mrs Harris is on Lindos Lady, and Mr Chan is on the pier!"

I jogged up the pier to Charlie and Carmen, who were seated, their legs hanging off the pier where Lindos Lady was moored. I came to a halt, panting out of breath, and inquired if Angel was on the boat. Carmen nodded. I called out to her, "Angel, are you there? ... Quick!"

She emerged from the cabin. Charlie and Carmen had picked up on my urgency and got up to join me, eager to know what was so important.

"Have you found something?" Charlie asked with enthusiasm as Angel approached us. I held up the manuscript as if it were a treasure.

"I believe this manuscript is, without a doubt, the most significant document in the history of the world."

With her sunglasses perched above raised eyebrows, Carmen cast a glance at Charlie and then Angel before remarking, "I think he's serious."

"Hold onto your socks ... It claims to be the word of God ... and was penned around 10,500 BC!" I paused to gauge their shocked reactions. "It teaches the utilisation of frequencies within the earth ... love ... and light..."

Angel gestured vaguely, struggling to grasp what I had just revealed. "Can you be more specific, Axis?"

"Okay, like it's written in ancient Hebrew, the language of the Old Testament, and it discusses genetically engineering the human inhabitants of Earth to a higher level of intellect ... It explicitly states that God, the same God as in all religions, originated from outer space ... It contends that the ozone layer was deliberately created by these extra-terrestrial visitors as a means to gauge humanity's progress."

"Wait," Charlie interjected, "What do you mean by 'gauge humanity's progress'? Is it implying that the ozone layer is artificial?"

"Yes, indeed. Ozone is a chemical layer that's currently being depleted due to our production of ozone-depleting substances. It suggests that we have reached a stage in our evolution where we possess the capability to harm both ourselves and the environment. The book goes on to suggest that the holes in the ozone layer will allow specific space radiation, usually filtered by it, to penetrate, affecting us ... This radiation will trigger specific synapses in the brain to activate ... and—"

"Enlightenment will occur on a grand scale. Fascinating. They embedded a cosmic trigger in our atmosphere to prepare us for their return. Because they foresaw our eventual evolution," Angel interjected.

"Whoa, that's quite mind-boggling," Charlie remarked.

"I know, I know," I agreed. "It also discusses the magnetic grid of the Earth ... They anticipated that by now, it would have shifted by three degrees. They claim it will correct itself during a planetary alignment in the next two years."

"And how will that impact us?" Carmen inquired.

"It could unleash incredible powers for those who comprehend and harness this kind of magic," I elaborated.

"Could you provide an example of this power, this magic?" Charlie asked.

"Sure, telekinesis, telepathy, heightened psychic abilities, you name it. Tapping into the Earth's magnetic grid would enable you to levitate massive stone blocks with just your hand."

Carmen had an epiphany. "So this might explain how the pyramids were constructed."

"It all sounds rather 'X-Files' to me, I'm afraid," Charlie admitted, stroking his chin. "Just to clarify, people living in areas affected by ozone depletion today are being exposed to radiation that activates previously unused portions of their brains. Is that correct?"

"Yes, we currently utilise only a small percentage of our brains," I affirmed.

"I've read books on that," Charlie acknowledged. "So, we're being subliminally enlightened to make us more receptive to these extra-terrestrial beings or God when he—"

Carmen interjected, "Or she..."

Charlie concluded, "Makes a grand appearance."

"Exactly," Carmen agreed, "Not too long ago, people were fearful of UFOs or UAPs, but not anymore..."

A profound silence enveloped us as we contemplated the magnitude of this hypothesis. Then Charlie spoke up, "You're absolutely right, Carmen. But let's continue ... Axis, are you saying that the Earth's magnetic grid is currently off by approximately three degrees?"

"Indeed it is, my friend. It's a well-documented fact," I confirmed.

"Yes, I recall now, I've read about that as well. Throughout history, the magnetic poles have shifted from their present positions several times. This means that the Earth's axis, no pun intended, has altered during various eras ... Now, if such a shift occurs in our time, every satellite, all navigation systems, mapping, and so on, would become entirely useless ... and that, my friends, spells chaos. You're also suggesting that this ancient power, a power that may have been present when the Earth was last in alignment thousands of years ago..."

I interjected to clarify, "Approximately 12,000 years ago, to be precise ... It is believed that it was disrupted by a collision with an asteroid, which likely triggered the great flood and the sinking of Atlantis..."

"That power is now on the brink of being made accessible to those who comprehend it today. Axis, what you're saying is that this manuscript provides evidence that a struggle between good and evil, as prophesied by Nostradamus, sages, prophets, mystics, philosophers ... and written in most ancient texts of organised religions ... will lead to the end of the world ... You're talking about

Armageddon!"

"In short, my friends, this manuscript must not fall into the wrong hands. I've only decoded 2% of it so far; I'm a novice, and AI is doing the heavy lifting. But if what I've uncovered is any indication ... well, whoever possesses it ... holds the key to the greatest power on Earth."

We all contemplated this notion, then Angel suggested, "What if the person holding the manuscript gains increased personal powers or something?"

Carmen playfully hummed the Twilight Zone theme, and we all exchanged concerned glances, wondering if we were somehow responsible.

"I'll try to decipher more of the text, but you may be right. If an evil individual were to possess it, their malevolence might indeed be amplified," I concluded.

"Do you grasp the implications of what you're saying, Axis ... Angel?" Charlie asked. "I mean, if this manuscript is as extraordinary and potent as you suggest, why was it concealed inside a sarcophagus in the jungles of San Pedro?"

We all exchanged uncertain glances, searching for an answer. Then I ventured, "Maybe it was waiting for Angel to find it?"

Later that day, I found myself alone on the porch, captivated by the most breathtaking sunset I had ever witnessed. The soft strains of Spanish guitar emanated from the barroom stereo, enhancing the sense of tropical tranquillity that enveloped me.

Footsteps on the wooden floorboards heralded Charlie's arrival. He took a seat in one of the director's chairs and asked, "Any further revelations?"

"I managed to decipher a bit more before I started to doze off," I began. "The manuscript mentions current events, like earthquakes, natural disasters, escalating signs of change, global warming ... conflicts ... and it references 'the power of three.'"

Charlie raised an eyebrow. "The power of three? Isn't that a common religious motif ... Father, the Son, and the Holy Ghost?"

"Yes, you're correct," I admitted. "I came down here to mull it over further ... In the Old Testament, you often find references to three angels ... the three wise men ... three crucifixions ... 666, the number of the beast, which is a multiple of three ... Twelve apostles. Then there's Pythagoras' perfect number: the magic number ... the sacred number. The manuscript hints at the existence of three books on Earth, concealed in three different locations."

"Three books?... and we possess one of the three, right?"

"I believe so," I affirmed.

"What if we had all three?"

"Then you'd win the lucky door prize!" We shared a laugh. "No, no, I'm not certain yet, but based on what I can gather, the three books need to be brought together at a specific place and time for a particular purpose ... something related to 'God's door.'"

"It's starting to sound like a quest straight out of Don Quixote or the search for the Holy Grail," Charlie remarked. "What does a fellow need to do to get a drink around here?"

"That's easy. Boy!" I called out, and Boy promptly appeared.

"Yes, sir?"

I gestured for Charlie to place the order.

"A couple of JD's on the rocks, please, Boy."

Always eager to assist, Boy grinned and hurried off to fulfil the request.

"I don't think this is merely a book, Charlie; it's a calling ... and I suspect Angel was chosen or ordained through some divine ceremony to fulfil a task or tasks, whatever they may be."

"Perhaps it involves collecting all three books? Do you think we were chosen to play a role in this quest?" Charlie quipped, feigning a look of dread in his eyes.

Boy returned with the drinks.

"Thank you, Boy," I said. "Cheers, big ears."

"Big ears?" Charlie protested.

"Oh, just something a person I knew would say, nothing personal."

"Oh Boy," Charlie called out before Boy could disappear back inside. "Have you seen Miss Carmen and Mrs Harris?"

Boy paused at the door and replied, "Yes, sir. Miss Carmen is with Miss Rita in the dining room, and Mrs Harris went to the ruins."

I shot out of my seat as if I had been stung by a bee on the behind. "What! ... Alone? Damn it!"

~ ~ ~

Angel perched on a rock near the temple ruins, taking a sip from her water bottle. The trek had been arduous in the humid conditions, compounded by the need to navigate around fallen trees and branches left by the hurricane. The path was already challenging due to the dense vegetation. Being athletically inclined, she had managed well, needing only a second wind to enter the ruins and retrieve Richard's remains.

~ ~ ~

I struggled to steer the worn-out ex-U.S Army truck, swerving to avoid various obstacles left behind by the hurricane along the dirt track leading to the mountains. Potholes filled with rainwater posed the primary hazard, and the road was slick. Charlie, riding shotgun, had initially found it amusing.

"Enjoying the ride so far, mate? Why don't you take the wheel yourself?" I quipped.

Before he could respond, we hit a sizable pothole, causing the truck to skid on the slippery road, nearly veering off the edge of a precipice. Charlie's prior amusement transformed into a white-knuckled grip on the seat as we came to a halt just inches from the cliff's edge. He gazed out of his window at the valley below, his complexion now pale.

"Not as amusing now, is it?"

"It's going to be precarious driving back in the dark. Are you sure this is a good idea, Axis?"

"We don't have much of a choice, Charlie. We can only hope the headlights hold up when we need them in the dark," I replied, though it concealed my awareness of the real danger.

~ ~ ~

Angel had brought along a longer rope, which she used to rappel into the shaft, retrieve Richard's remains, and carefully pack them into a sack. As she ascended to the top of the well, hauling the sack, she was startled by the sound of applause. She pulled the sack over the well's edge and scanned her surroundings, searching for the source of the clapping.

In the shadows, a dark figure moved about twenty metres away from her and called out, "Well done, Angie, well done." The male voice echoed through the cavernous ruins.

Angel continued securing Richard's remains and, as she retrieved the rope from the well, the sharp crack of a gunshot and a bullet ricocheting off a column only a metre away from her made her freeze.

"Now, let's be reasonable about this, Angie. Richard has been resting down there comfortably for the past ten years. I don't see why he has to leave now. What do you think, Richard? What's your opinion, Richard? Speak up; I can't hear you, bonehead."

"Get out of here, Mike. I don't want to see your face! You've caused me enough pain!"

He erupted into raucous, cynical laughter. "Pain! Huh! Pain? You've got no idea how much pain you and your pathetic husband caused me."

The imposing figure of Mike Ong, obscured in the shadows and moving with a noticeable limp, stopped just two metres from her. Angel aimed her torchlight at his face, but what she saw repelled her. His face bore grotesque disfigurements, and in the fading light, he looked like a terrifying monster.

CHAPTER
THIRTEEN

"Yes, it's me. But you only recognised me because I called you Angie, didn't you?"

In a flash, he grabbed her and pulled her close. "How about a kiss, baby? What, I'm not handsome enough anymore? Not attracted to me because your sweet Richard burnt my fucking face off!"

He snatched a fistful of her hair and brought her in close to inspect his grotesque face.

"Why not, Angie! Didn't you once tell me that beauty has nothing to do with looks ... it all comes from within..."

She struggled against his grip and shouted, "Let go of me, Mike!"

He pulled her even closer and tried to kiss her. She sharply turned her face away from him.

"Come on, Angie baby, just like old times."

She pretended to give in to him ... Once again, he tried to kiss her. She brought her knee up into his groin ... The pain almost crippled him, and he let go. While he was writhing in pain, she hurriedly grabbed the bag and made a run for it.

A man stepped out from behind cover, grabbed her by the hair, and dragged her back to Ong. She immediately recognised him; it was Dino, the bent cop.

"Your little angel here was trying to fly away," he informed Ong.

The pain had left Ong infuriated. "Fancy you and your friends believing we'd do a deal with you. I want this estate. It's mine!"

With Dino restraining her, Ong slapped her hard across the face.

"Mine, you hear!" he yelled insanely and then ordered, "Kill her!"

Her lip bleeding from the assault, Angel snarled, "You always were a coward, Mike. Why don't you do your own dirty work?"

He whipped out a switchblade, flicked it open menacingly, put the blade against her cheek, and snarled, "How about a cosmetic make-over to match mine?"

With all her might, she elbowed Dino in the stomach and wrenched herself free, and with blood seeping from a cut on her cheek, she took off as fast as her legs could carry her.

~ ~ ~

The truck shuddered to a stop beside Angel's jeep. Charlie and I got out, a sense of trouble hanging in the air. "Something's wrong, I can feel it," I said, my senses on high alert.

A shot rang out. "That came from the ruins," I said urgently, leading Charlie quickly into the jungle toward the Temple.

As we broke through the bushes, I ran into Angel. After the initial shock, I clutched her shoulders. She had a frantic look in her eyes.

"What's wrong? I heard a shot."

"It's Mike ... Ong!"

Charlie pulled his pistol. Another shot sounded, and the bullet scored a tree trunk right next to us.

Charlie shouted, "Take cover!"

We crouched in hiding, and Charlie asked, "Is it just Ong?"

"No, Dino is with him. I don't know if there are others," Angel said.

"We better make for the jeep," I said, and they both nodded. I raised my index finger to signal the plan: 1, then 2, then 3! We jumped up, and leading the way, we took off like a bat out of hell. Shots rang out, narrowly missing us. We reached the clearing and found the jeep.

"I'll take the truck," Charlie yelled.

"No, it's too slow," I said and jumped into the jeep behind the wheel. Angel got in beside me.

We could hear them coming.

"Go!" Charlie yelled.

We sped off, leaving a cloud of dust behind us. Meanwhile, Ong emerged from the jungle, realising he had lost his targets. He climbed into the truck and attempted to start it, but Charlie was already lurking behind his seat, pistol in hand.

"Mr Ong, I presume," Charlie said formally. "We finally meet. Did Mr Raman fail to pass on my message to you?"

A menacing click signalled a gun's hammer being cocked. Charlie raised his hands in surrender. Dino, positioned at the back window with his pistol, had the drop on him.

"Hmm, I guess he did," Charlie said with resignation. Ong swiftly disarmed him, and with the gun aimed at him ordered, "Get out of the truck. I think Dino has a score to settle with you."

As Charlie set a foot on the ground, Dino pistol-whipped him across the side of the head.

I slowed the jeep, pounding my hands on the steering wheel in frustration.

"No! I don't like it!" I shouted.

Angel urged, "Go back then!"

I executed a wild reverse U-turn, splashing through a puddle, and roared off back to the truck.

We pulled up in the clearing, and the truck was there, but there was no-one in sight. I turned to Angel with a determined expression.

"No arguments, right. I want you to take the truck back to the hotel. I'll get Charlie, then call you on the radio."

I could see she was about to object, but I raised my hand, gesturing for her to stop.

"It's not about your ability, Angel; it's about your importance. We need you to stay alive. Alright?"

She leaned across and gave me a surprise kiss on the cheek.

"You pick the wildest time to get romantic," I teased.

She hopped out and, before going to the truck, said with a cheeky grin, "That wasn't romantic, loco, that was 'be careful.' Romantic is something completely different."

I raised an eyebrow, intrigued, and replied, "Wow, I can hardly wait to test out that theory."

She stepped up into the truck, started it, and drove off. I ran for the cover of the jungle, making my way stealthily toward the ruins.

I sneakily stalked into the temple, moving cautiously toward the well. Suddenly, from out of nowhere, I was struck from behind and then literally hoisted into the well. Dino picked up the bag containing Richard's remains and scurried off into the jungle.

~ ~ ~

I woke up in almost pitch darkness and fumbled in my pocket for my cigarette lighter. As I flicked it on, I winced when it illuminated a person sitting opposite me with his back against the wall.

"Charlie," I said, relieved to see a familiar face.

"Glad you could drop in. Lucky you landed on me or you might have broken something," he said facetiously.

"There's a Confucian proverb in that somewhere," I joked. "You alright, mate?"

"Just a pounding headache and a few bruises. I'll live ... provided we ever get out of here."

I struggled to my feet and looked up. "Now that I think we can do, but not this way."

Charlie stood up, holding the arch of his back. "You're not exactly exuding confidence, oh senior one."

"Sorry about that, but it's the best I can do right now. Follow me."

I led him along the narrow corridor and then stopped at the dead end.

"What now?" Charlie asked sceptically, staring at the end wall.

The doorway was still slightly ajar from when Angel and I had been through it. I pushed it open enough for Charlie to squeeze through. "Can you fit?" I joked.

Sucking in his stomach, he squeezed out. "Steady, old son. This isn't the time for fat jokes."

Once inside the chamber, I held up the lighter for Charlie to see the sarcophagus. He was amazed. "Wow! It's one thing talking about it, but a whole other universe seeing it in the flesh!"

"Help me get it open."

Once we had it open, I held the lighter close to the death mask for him to see. "Angel!" Charlie said, aghast. "You were so right; she's the spitting image."

The light was flickering and burning my fingers. I reached in and took hold of the mummy's left arm and ripped it out of the socket.

"Whoa! What are you doing, man?"

"I'm sorry, my dear," I told the mummy as I touched the mummified hand with the naked flame of the lighter and set it afire.

"That's handy," Charlie quipped.

I was relieved to pocket the lighter. The flaming hand had lit up the inside of the tomb.

"Next we need to find an exit. Most tombs have more than one … well, so Howard Carter said anyway."

"That was in the Valley of the Kings," Charlie reminded me.

I spoke with my best Confucian accent, "Do not worry, oh honourable number one friend. Watch carefully so that you might learn from the master."

"Yeah, right," Charlie scoffed.

After a quick scan of the surrounding walls, I moved back to the sarcophagus. I waved the burning hand around the outside of the pedestal, stopped once satisfied, and pushed the sarcophagus. It moved. "See, there's a breeze coming from here moving the flame about; help me."

We pushed the sarcophagus until it revealed an opening beneath it.

"Pay dirt, I think."

"Brilliant, oh grand master … This day shall be marked in history as the day of Axis Stone and the flaming arm."

I hopped up onto the pedestal and stepped into the narrow shaft. "Follow me if you can fit."

The pit had a tunnel leading off with a low ceiling. I crouched down and followed it, knowing my hand-torch was rapidly running out of fuel, and the smoke from it was filling the tunnel. After about twenty metres, the flame had burnt down to my fingers, and I had to drop it. We were amazed by what we saw.

"Shame about the cliché, but there's a light at the end of the tunnel," I said. When we reached the exit shaft, we looked up the six metres or so, and Charlie said, "Pity we didn't bring our platform shoes from the seventies."

"You'll need to get onto my shoulders to climb out, then throw me down a vine or something."

~ ~ ~

Meanwhile, a car engine roared. Ong's Pajero was seriously bogged; the wheels were just spinning. Dino got out, and in the headlights, unfurled a cable from the winch at the front of the vehicle. He walked it to a tree and fastened it around its girth. Job done, he gave Ong the thumbs up. The winch laboured, and then the Pajero slowly emerged from the bog.

Charlie and I were spying on Ong and Dino from the cover of the jungle. They drove off without seeing us. We made for the jeep, and as soon as we reached it, I called Angel on the two-way.

"Angel, are you there? Over."

We waited, and there was only static. Then, to our relief, came Angel's voice.

"I'm here, yes, go ahead … over."

"We're on our way, but Ong and Dino are ahead of us. Take Carmen, Rita, and the others and get on the boat. Anchor offshore; you'll be safe there … understand? Over."

"Roger that. Too much ozone. Out."

I looked at Charlie mystified, "What do you suppose she meant by that?"

He was just as confused, "Too much ozone? It has to be a reference to what you found in the manuscript."

"Yes, but what?"

~ ~ ~

Angel put down the microphone and looked forlornly at Carmen. Standing with the manuscript in one hand and a gun in the other aimed at them, Vitale smirked at Rita beside him.

"If you're right, babe ... and this book is the only one in the world, we might just have ourselves a fortune ... Antiquities are a hot commodity, you know."

"Sad to see you back running with the pack, Rita," Angel said.

"Listen, sister, that book is my meal ticket. I've paid my dues, so I figure I've earned it."

"Even if it's at the expense of millions of lives? The book will bring a curse on you, Vitale," Angel warned.

"I don't give a damn about all your end-of-the-world, suspicious, crap," Vitale snarled. "That only matters to whoever wants to buy the book. So, here's what we're gonna do—"

~ ~ ~

I was pushing the jeep like it was a cross-country rally. We could see Ong's tail-lights up ahead. The road flattened out, which gave me the chance to close the gap, I trod on the gas. Charlie foraged through the glove compartment and found a pair of binoculars and a flare gun. One shot only, but he was satisfied.

Dino looked out the rear window and said, "It must be them. They're closing on us."

Ong glanced at the rear-view mirror from driving. "How the hell did they get out of the well? Shoot now ... and ask questions later."

Dino wound down the window, leaned out, and fired a round at the jeep.

CHAPTER
FOURTEEN

Vitale and Tong were walking Angel and Carmen at gunpoint toward the end of the pier. "Stop," Vitale commanded. "Take off your clothes."

Carmen defiantly put her fists on her hips and smirked at him. "That's just not going to happen, Vinny."

Vitale fired a shot into the wooden floor right next to her foot. They knew he meant business and so acquiesced, stripping down to their undergarments.

"Take her onto the boat and tie her to it," Vitale ordered Tong.

The big man obeyed and dragged Angel kicking and protesting onto the Lindos Lady. Vitale prodded his pistol into Carmen's back and moved her into the work-shed.

~ ~ ~

We heard a gunshot, and I immediately swerved the jeep while Charlie ducked.

"I got it. Angel said too much ozone. It was a warning."

Charlie screwed up his nose, "What are you going on about?"

"Angel ... Vitale must be there. You know, with less ozone, people are enlightened, with more, they're not. Vitale could never be enlightened, so she said there was too much ozone. Clever."

"Man, that's so obscure," Charlie said. "Tailgate them up real close."

I stepped on it and closed right up on them. Dino was leaning out of the window and got a bead on Charlie. But before he could pull the trigger, Charlie fired the flare. It shot like a missile into the back of Ong's Pajero and ignited, setting the rear of the vehicle ablaze. I swerved and pulled up in a broadside. The Pajero only made it a little further down the road before the gas tank exploded into a massive fireball.

We watched Dino and Ong incinerated in the inferno.

~ ~ ~

Both Angel and Carmen were tied up in the cabin of Lindos Lady. Carmen was hanging from her bound hands unconscious, her face bleeding.

Tong opened the cowling on the inboard motors, leaned inside, and removed the bungs. The boat began to fill with water. Vitale was watching from the pier.

"You're scum, Vitale!" Angel called out. "There was no need to abuse her!"

"Cast off, Tong," Vitale ordered ruthlessly.

Tong leapt onto the pier, cast off the bow line, then the stern. He then gave the boat a big shove with his foot. It drifted out to sea with the outgoing tide.

Vitale smiled macabrely, continuing to listen to Angel screaming.

"You'll be sorry, Vitale! You'll pay for this with your life!"

He and Tong turned their backs on the Lindos Lady and began making their way back along the pier. "She'll be a real Angel soon."

At the front desk, Boy and Cora had also been stripped to their underclothes and were tied and gagged, standing facing one another. They were both most embarrassed by their awkward predicament.

The two-way radio crackled in the office. "Angel, are you there? Angel, it's Axis, come in? Over."

Boy spoke even while gagged, "We need to get the radio. You must walk in time with me."

Cora nodded, understanding his muffled speech. With their legs bound together, they had to synchronize their steps. They made it into the office.

"Hello, anyone there? It's Axis. Over."

Boy stretched his fingers to try and flick open the microphone. Finally, he reached it.

I had the mike in one hand, while steering with the other. "Is there anyone there! Damn! Over!"

Then came a muffled, illegible response. It repeated a little more discernibly, "Vitale, hurry." Then came static.

"Did you hear that?"

Charlie nodded, "Yes, it sounded like Boy."

I put my foot flat to the floor.

Tong had the power cord of the radio in his hand. Vitale grinned at Boy and Cora. "I figured you'd call them, thanks. Goodnight, kids."

He flicked off the light, leaving Boy and Cora in their uncompromising position in the dark. Tong shut the office door behind them.

"Get the car, Tong, I'll get Rita." He headed upstairs.

Carmen had regained consciousness and was using her toes to try and untie the knot holding Angel bound. Water was lapping their feet—the boat was sinking. They were a hundred metres from shore.

"Come on baby, you can do it," Angel encouraged Carmen.

Through clenched teeth, her face bloody, Carmen said, "This definitely wasn't in my job description."

Vitale entered Rita's hotel room, looked around, couldn't see her, and then heard water splashing in the bathroom. He found her taking a bubble bath.

"Come on in, big boy," Rita purred flirtatiously.

He sat on the edge of the bathtub. "You've always been a naughty dame, Rita."

"Only with you, Vinny-pie."

"Oh yeah ... What about that guy... what was it, Bristo? Anyhow, you remember him. It was a few weeks before we came here..."

Her attitude changed, "I don't like the sound of this, Vinny.

Where's it going?"

He dragged his pistol barrel through the bubbles, carving a line from her neck to her navel.

"You know, I didn't like being given the bullet. So, it's an eye for an eye … I've got a bullet for you."

Rita sat up in a panic and screamed, "No! Vinny! No!! The book … I helped you … No!"

One shot, and the bathwater turned scarlet.

In the limo, Tong looked up from filing his fingernails hearing the gunshot. He knew Rita had just departed the land of the living. At the same time, he failed to notice Carmen and Angel emerge from the water and run behind the car. They entered the rear entrance of the hotel.

Vitale casually made his way down the stairs, wiping Rita's blood off his face with a handkerchief. He stopped at the front desk and collected the manuscript from where he'd hidden it. The lobby was dimly lit by one light.

"That book isn't for you, Vitale."

Vitale's carefree mood vanished. He swiftly drew his pistol and scanned the lobby. "Angel? Where the heck are you?"

The lights went out. If there's one thing that Vitale despised the most, it's darkness.

I turned off the headlights and stealthily rolled the jeep to the edge of the road, a hundred metres from the hotel. I could see Vitale's limousine parked in front on the forecourt.

"I think someone's in the limo," Charlie said. "Wait." He rummaged through the glove compartment and found the binoculars. He surveyed the limo. "It's Tong," he confirmed.

Vitale had his gun aimed at Boy and Cora, still bound together. He shouted, "Turn the lights on and show yourself by the time I count to ten … or I'll shoot Boy and Cora with one shot …. and you know I'm not joking. One … two … three … four…."

"Alright, Vitale, you win … I'm coming out … but I can't turn on the lights … it must be a fuse."

Vitale moved to the centre of the lobby floor, pistol ready. A 'crunch' came from behind him, and he turned sharply. He turned back again, horrified to find the Major rolling out of the darkness toward him in a wheelchair. He fired four shots into Roland's lifeless body, but it kept on coming. He turned again, and this time Paddy came at him from a different direction in a wheelchair. He fired at him, then, click! click! He was out of ammo. Paddy stopped and fell out of the wheelchair onto the floor. Angel was behind Paddy, armed with a kitchen knife. Vitale backed in a panic toward the front door.

"You don't have it in you," he barked, uncertain.

"I wouldn't be so sure, Vinny. I've gutted plenty of fish."

He turned and raced out through the front door.

Tong was behind the wheel. I surprised him, pulled open the door, reached in, and dragged him out. We exchanged blows, then he pulled a switchblade—he flicked it open—it was a big switchblade—and he knew how to use it. He slashed at me, slicing my forearm open.

Thinking on the fly, I ripped the antenna off the back of the limo and then whipped it across Tong's face. We parried ... Tong lunged with the blade. I delivered a deadly right-hand chin-jab into his throat. He went down and landed on his own blade.

Vitale ran out from the hotel and skidded to a halt when he saw me standing over Tong on the ground. Charlie walked out from behind the limo. Angel and Carmen emerged from the hotel.

In a panic, Vitale ran out into the middle of the forecourt, clutching the book against his chest.

"You can't have it. I've got all the power ... Rita told me ... I know all about it ... It's mine, I tell ya!"

There was a full moon, big and yellow in the clear sky. In the moonlight, Vitale caught a glimpse of Lindos Lady at the end of the pier. He figured to make a run for it. Angel and I went after him. He was well ahead of us.

When Vitale reached the end of the pier, a bright beam of light appeared from out of the night sky and engulfed him. He stopped dead, frozen in his tracks by its awesome power. It was so bright we had to stop and shield our eyes. At least I did, Angel didn't seem affected.

I pulled my sunglasses out of my pocket, put them on, and searched the sky for the source of the otherworldly beam of light. But it didn't appear to have a source. The laser-like column of bright yellow light simply extended up into the sky and beyond.

I looked back at Vitale in time to see his clothes catch fire. Then, his skin began to melt off his body. He was standing frozen in time, transformed by the light into a silent, molten, human sculpture.

Angel walked toward the light as though hypnotically drawn to it.

I tried to stop her, but she pulled away. It was then I somehow knew it was meant to be.

She stepped into the beam, and once engulfed by it, she glowed like an angel. She removed the book from Vitale's clawed hands and then calmly walked out of the beam back to me.

The light retracted, leaving Angel with the book glowing fluorescent blue from head to toe. The blue aura faded. I held out my arms, and she fell into them unconscious. Charlie removed the book from her. I picked her up and carried her into the hotel.

~ ~ ~

Carmen lay in bed, her face red, blistered, and peeling from exposure to the radiation in the beam. Charlie emerged from the bathroom in blue and white striped pyjamas, brushing his teeth. His face was also red, blistered, and peeling.

"Sharing your bed was certainly not in the job description, Mr Chan," Carmen quipped.

"It is now," he mumbled past the toothbrush in his mouth. He removed it. "What are we going to do about this shedding? I feel like a lizard."

"You look like one," she said, then burst into giggles.

"Have you looked in a mirror lately, Miss reptilicus?"

The house phone rang, and Carmen answered it. "Hi, sure, we'll be down in twenty."

CHAPTER
FIFTEEN

It was a beautiful sunny morning, and I was having breakfast on the porch. My left forearm was bandaged, and my face was blistered, making me look like I'd survived a plane crash in the Sahara Desert and a six-day hike in blistering heat to civilization.

Angel appeared on the porch, dressed in a flowing white cotton dress. Her face was clear, with no blisters or peeling. She gave me a delicate kiss on the lips and looked deeply into my eyes while stroking the side of my blistered face with her index finger. She seemed different to me, no longer the tomboy but delicate, like a flower.

"I love you, Axis Stone," she said softly. I wasn't usually one to react well to the 'L' word, but coming from her, with this total change in her demeanour, it seemed perfectly natural. However, I couldn't bring myself to reciprocate, it would mean breaking my code of ethics.

"You look gorgeous this morning," I chose thus avoiding talk of love. "I must apologise for my appearance; I seem to be shedding my skin. Must be that time of the month," I joked.

"How's your arm?"

"Reminds me of the mummy. It'll be fine; you did a great job patching me up, doc."

She sat and gazed out to sea with a distant look in her eyes. Boy brought glasses of fresh orange juice for us. He too noticed the drastic change in Angel and couldn't quite take his eyes off her. She seemed somehow radiant.

"That hurricane sure brought winds of change," Boy remarked.

"Cora mentioned to me this morning that you proposed to her last night while you were tied together," I said smugly, jealous that he wasn't peeling. He blushed.

"Um, it felt like the right thing to do, sir, under the circumstances."

I found that funny, but Angel continued to stare blankly at the view. Charlie and Carmen arrived and took seats.

"Morning. Did we all sleep well, sunburn and all?" Charlie said with a chuckle. "Hey, will you look at Angel? She isn't sunburnt!"

"We need to talk," I said seriously.

Angel changed her focus to Charlie, "Hello Charlie, and Carmen, I love you."

I was a little relieved that her pledge of love for me now seemed to be magnanimous. Charlie and Carmen seemed a little rattled by it.

"Yes, we certainly need to talk ... I've been pondering that light all night. It incinerated old Vitale but seemed to have no effect on Angel at all. In fact, we're more affected by it than she is, and she stepped right into it."

"I believe the light was divine, Charlie, possibly God's door as the manuscript mentioned. Maybe it originated from space through a portal. You see, I think Angel was chosen, perhaps thousands of years ago, to be the custodian of the manuscript at this particular point in time. Maybe she has fulfilled this role at other times in the past. You saw the face of the mummy. She has been having dreams since she can remember, all related to this divine destiny. In these dreams, she sees herself in different times, always a woman, always fighting to preserve the manuscript."

"As sceptical as I might be, I can't deny what we witnessed last night ... not after seeing that," Charlie admitted.

"Are you suggesting that Angel is reincarnated?" Carmen inquired.

"Perhaps ... Look, I've managed to decipher a bit more of the manuscript since yesterday ... but, I don't mean to freak you guys out, but it's getting seriously bizarre. It's now mentioning us by name and it accurately described what happened last night!"

"Come on, man, you said it was written thousands of years ago," Charlie exclaimed, clearly bewildered by this revelation.

"And the really strange part is—"

"Don't tell me it can get even stranger," Charlie interrupted.

"It alters itself daily ... the text does. It's like it's writing itself. At the same time, it seems to speak to my inner mind while I'm reading it. Look, I'm just a private investigator, you know what that entails. I'm no academic and certainly no archaeologist ... I attempted to decipher the manuscript only because there was no-one else here to do it. I used an AI app to translate it ... one word at a time. It was a slow and tedious process. But after last night, everything changed. I can now read it as if it's written in English. Something must have affected me ... I mean, it affected Angel. Look at her ... she's hardly said a word, and I doubt she can even hear me."

"Maybe you've been spending too much time—" Charlie began.

Carmen cut him off, saying, "Don't even go there, Charlie ... What does the book say, Axis?"

Suddenly, Angel snapped out of her trance and grabbed Carmen's hand. Then she took hold of my hand with her other hand. As if compelled by some strange force, Charlie took my other hand and joined hands with Carmen. It was a peculiar Kumbaya moment, and then Angel spoke.

"We are beings of light. We have been enlightened. We have a message of light to convey to the people of the world. Change is imminent. We are meant to facilitate that change. It is time for the Earth, its inhabitants, and the cosmos to be in harmony as one. But first, we must uncover the next icon..."

We each contemplated her words for a solemn moment, then she said, "The manuscript states that three divine icons must be unearthed and brought together in a sacred place to harness the power of three. This must occur before the alignment—the three-degree magnetic north shift. We possess the first icon, the manuscript itself. It will guide us to the next, and so forth."

"What is the next icon?" Charlie asked.

Then Carmen said, "Where is it? Why is all of this happening to us?"

Angel responded, "We can only be divine when we are in tune with each other ... and in harmony with Mother Earth."

~ ~ ~

It had been a sombre farewell. We all felt that we'd had an illuminating experience, not akin to a trip to Tibet, but a genuinely unearthly encounter that had etched its mark on each of us in unique ways. Angel was finally at peace with herself, Carmen finally comprehended her job description, and Charlie, well, I don't know about Charlie; he seemed to take it all in his stride. As for me, I think perhaps, aside from Angel, I had been the most profoundly affected. I had read the manuscript, but it wasn't in a normal manner—the book virtually read itself to me and I'd have to say that was a very surreal experience. It was disconcerting enough that I had shared the same vision of a battle in the distant past as Angel, something that I suppose could be attributed to some form of shared subconscious connection, but the outcome of it—no, that couldn't simply be explained away.

The manuscript? Well, that remained in the safekeeping of Angel. We had all agreed that she was the custodian of it, as well as being the driving force behind recovering the two other items to complete the sacred trio. Had we experienced turning the key that had unlocked God's door? None of us could come to a definitive conclusion on that question. The most significant question left unanswered was whether we, as a team, were meant to pursue the quest or if it was solely up to Angel. The one thing we did concur on was that only time would reveal the answer.

I had received a call from Kendy, informing me that things were piling up in my absence, so it was time for me to bid farewell to the other three. I had expected it to be difficult when it came to Angel, but it turned out not to be. She was confident that we would soon reunite—destiny, she claimed.

After an hour of providing a statement to the police and then forensics arriving to sweep the place, a vehicle arrived to remove the bodies of Roland, Rita, Tong, and the vitrified remains of Vitale, which still stood in a strange pose at the end of the pier. Good luck to forensics with that one. They'd already bagged the bodies of Dino and Ong from the burnt-out vehicle on the main road. It had been carnage.

~ ~ ~

The bus ride along the dirt track back to San Pedro didn't feel as jarring as it had on my initial journey; perhaps I had become acclimatised. I remember gazing out of the window at the mountain range, knowing that in the jungle lay the remnants of a lost city that a man had sacrificed his life to uncover. I half-expected Tears for Fears to play on the bus radio again, but in this instance, we had possibly thwarted the villains' attempt to rule the world, or at least this pristine part of the world, for the time being.

~ ~ ~

The cold night air gnawed at me like a crocodile's teeth as I returned to NYC. Thankfully, I had my cashmere overcoat, which I had lugged to and from the Caribbean, to provide some relief from the biting chill.

I had only been away for a week, but it felt like a month. The worst part was contemplating how I would explain what had happened to Kendy; she would surely think I had lost my mind.

The next morning, I arrived at the office and was surprised to find myself there early. Kendy arrived right on the dot of nine, bearing croissants.

"Well, hey, I didn't expect you to beat me here," Kendy chirped.

"I figured I'd get the coffee brewing in anticipation of a croissant," I replied.

While she hung her coat on the rack, I poured us both coffees, and within seconds, the warmth of the coffee and croissants began to thaw us out. Kendy settled on the sofa, ready for my report.

An hour and two more coffees later, Kendy's eyes were as wide as dinner plates. I had expected a reaction, but I never anticipated Kendy being at a loss for words.

"I know it's hard to believe, but I swear, that's what happened," I said.

"You could have been imitating Rod Serling, and I would have believed it was an episode of the Twilight Zone. Seriously, man, write that story up ... it'll sell as science fiction," Kendy exclaimed.

"Tell me about it. Look at my face; this isn't sunburn."

"A light from space that melts this guy Vitale, Angel steps into it unscathed, while all the others have radiation burns, a coffin with a corpse that's the spitting image of Angel, who is clutching a twelve-thousand-year-old book in her clawed hands ... a book that later starts speaking to you, and to top it all off, it writes itself."

"Yeah, and let's not forget about the visions..."

"Oh yeah, visions of you and Angel in a sword-and-sandal battle, where she gets impaled on a spear or something ... Geez, and I thought the last case was out of this world! This one's from another galaxy. "So, is that it, all like done and dusted?" Kendy inquired.

"I wish I could say yes, but I have a nagging suspicion there's more to come," I replied.

Kendy got up and gestured toward the new gadget. "Let me introduce you to our new answering machine, which, on my last count, has recorded five new briefs wanting to be solved, along with one rather irate individual named Bella, wondering why you hadn't shown up in L.A. like you apparently mentioned."

"I didn't say that. It was just a passing thought ... one that I must have mentioned to Carlos, who's obviously spilled the beans."

"He's a cop, boss. Cops aren't known for keeping secrets."

The landline rang. "You take that call; I'm not quite ready to face the world yet. It might be Bella."

Kendy shot me a look that clearly said, 'You wimp,' before picking up the phone.

"Hello, Stone Investigations, Kendy Lee speaking ... Hello?... Oh, sorry, it must be a bad connection. Yes, he's back. Who's calling? Oh, Mrs Harris. Axis mentioned you. My condolences for your father-in-law."

Kendy gave me a questioning 'take it' look, and I nodded. She said her goodbyes and then handed me the phone.

"Hey Angel, how are you? They're still with you, huh? Yes, I received it, but I haven't had a chance to check my email yet. I'll call you. Take care and say hi to Charlie and Carmen. Yes, it's freezing here. I know where I'd rather be. I understand that. Thank you."

"Must have been stunning there," Kendy commented.

"Quite magical, water so clear it was like glass ... idyllic ... if you were to look up the words 'tropical resort' in the dictionary there should a photo of Lindos."

"So what did she want?"

Charlie and Carmen are staying on because Angel has had another vision."

"About?"

"Don't know. She couldn't say ... she dictated it to Carmen, who emailed it to me for interpretation. She said it's too complicated to explain over the phone."

"Ah, Mr Stone, a new talent? Dream decoder, shall we add that to our letterhead?"

"Not until I've read the email," I replied with a hint of humour.

"Well, before you do, how about listening to these new cases?" Kendy suggested.

CHAPTER
SIXTEEEN

Kendy and I finished listening to the answering machine.

"I must admit the quality is better than my vintage unit."

"Yeah, the voices are actually clear," Kendy said sarcastically.

"Don't rub it in. So, there's only one case that interests me out of the five on offer..."

"Let me guess; the guy who thinks his wife, who had been abducted, came back as an alien?"

"No, that one's definitely a pass. The woman whose husband claims to be hearing voices because the military implanted him with a chip."

"I don't know about that; it sounded a bit weird," Kendy admitted.

"Hey Kendy, they were all pretty weird. That's what social media has done to the PI game nowadays. No more marital cheating cases, thank God, they can be solved by checking hubby's Facebook account; no need to hire a gumshoe."

"A gumshoe?"

"Yeah, that's what they used to call us ... back in the 1950s. It meant creeping around in quiet rubber shoes—a gumshoe."

"Did you ever do any of those cases, like spying on cheaters?" Kendy asked.

"When I first started, that's all I did."

She was grinning like a Cheshire cat. "I wouldn't mind taking on one of those cases. Maybe I should get a PI license."

"I think you should. Look into it; I don't know the ropes these days, especially here in NYC ... how about you do that while I read this email from Carmen."

"What about the guy with the voices?"

"Get back to him and set up an appointment."

Kendy went to her office, and I sat down behind my desk and opened my laptop.

An hour later, Kendy popped out of her office and announced, "Danny Spence, his wife Miranda and the people in his head will be here tomorrow at ten A.M., okay? ... Axis?"

Kendy picked up on my distraction from the email I'd read.

"Oh, sorry Kendy ... ten in the morning, the voices, um, Danny, fine."

"Something in the email got you thinking?"

"Yeah, Angel had a vision of another battle..."

"Sword and sandal?"

"No, this time it was recent ... she figured it was in the Middle East. She saw herself again, and the same guy that seems to be in all her visions ... this time they were on opposite sides. She was a guerrilla mercenary of some kind, and she thinks he was a Navy Seal."

"Is that all?"

"No, she said it was recurring ... the same dream over and over all night ... a battle, they confront one another and recognise they know each other ... there's chaos going on all around them, bombs, grenades, they're in the thick of battle—he tries to tell her something but he gets hit before he can finish ... something about Genesis."

"Genesis? ... Like in the Bible?"

"Don't know ... that was all. You see, last time, I was in the same vision as hers, which meant we could compare notes. But this time the vision is only hers. I need more detail."

Kendy sat on the sofa to think. "Maybe give her a call?"

"She doesn't want to talk over the phone."

She had an idea and sat on the edge of the sofa, excited. "Let's make a list of questions, like a questionnaire, then send it to Carmen ... from what you told me of her and Charlie, they'll buy into the research."

"Good thinking. Let's do it."

~ ~ ~

By late afternoon, Carmen had replied with all the questionnaire answers. Still feeling a little jet-lagged, I decided to call it a day and take the list of thirty questions and answers home to mull over.

~ ~ ~

That night, I awoke in a sweat from a vivid dream that I believed was influenced by Angel's answers to the questions. It was 3 AM, and I sat on the couch sipping on a JD, with recall images racing through my mind. I wasn't sure if I'd had a vision like Angel had, or if it was just a dream. Whatever the case, I had gleaned a lot more detail from the dream than I had from the questionnaire.

I got into the office just after nine, and Kendy was already there.

"Morning," she called from her office and then got up to bring me a croissant as I settled in behind my desk.

"Ran late ... I expected to be the early bird again, but waking up after a vivid dream in the middle of the night affected my plans, and I nodded back off at 4 AM, and then woke up late."

Pouring a couple of coffees, Kendy said, "That's cool; you probably needed to sleep off the jet lag anyway. So, what was the dream? Oh, before you tell me, Carmen sent through an email. Charlie brought in a palaeographer to help finish interpreting the manuscript."

"Oh yeah, a palaeographer? Did you Google him?"

"Hmm, hmm, she's Malaysian, from Kuala Lumpur; Dr Jax De Ville ... graduated Berkeley with honours ... published a paper last year; 'Lost Civilizations of the Pacific and the Sumerian Cuneiform Connection,' which was acclaimed by her academic peers."

"That's great; Charlie knows what he's doing. Only good can come of that. When does she get there?"

"Today, I think," Kendy replied.

"It's a big trip from KL," I noted.

"So, tell me about this dream."

I got up from my desk and went to the sofa, where I reclined like on a psychiatrist's couch. Kendy picked up on the vibe and pulled up a chair opposite, holding her digital voice recorder.

I closed my eyes and was transported back to the dream. Before I knew it, there was a knock at the door, and I sat up sharply.

"Who's that?" I asked.

"Oh hell, it'd be your ten o'clock with the Spences," Kendy replied.

I got up. "Time just flew by," I said as Kendy went to get the door.

She ushered in two individuals in their early sixties. Danny, with his long hair, had a distinct hippie look about him, and he was in a wheelchair. Miranda, his wife, appeared Asian, possibly Filipino. Danny appeared visibly nervous as Kendy asked Miranda to take a seat, and then she introduced me.

I tried to ease his nerves. "Well, Dan, can I call you that?" He nodded. "How did you learn about Stone Investigations?"

Miranda answered for him. Despite her Filipino accent, she obviously had been in the U.S. for a long time and spoke with fluency. She was a bit plump but had a pleasant demeanour. "We live in the house next door to Mr Booker. We've been friends for over thirty years, and sometimes he has drinks with Danny, so..."

"Ah, I've known Book since I was a kid; he worked with my parents."

"We moved in next door when Danny got out of the hospital the first time, after serving in the Gulf War."

"A veteran of the Iraq War ... a landmine took out my ability to ever walk again," Danny explained bitterly.

"He was lucky not to lose his life," Miranda added supportively.

"Sometimes I wish I had," Danny confessed, his eyes tearing up.

Recognising the man's distress, Kendy jumped in. "Can I interest you both in freshly brewed coffee and a chocolate donut?"

Miranda smiled and stood. "Sure can, let me help you, dear."

While the two ladies prepared morning tea, I probed a bit deeper with Danny.

"Tell me about the problem, Danny, and how you think I can help."

He composed himself. "Sorry about that, Mr Stone. I can get stressed sometimes."

"Understandable, Dan. Call me Axis."

"Book said I wouldn't have to pull any punches with you and that you'd understand, so I'll tell you straight what I think."

"Good, Dan, go ahead."

"After the landmine, I spent a few days in a MASH unit, then I was transferred onto the USS Comfort and eventually MEDVAC'd back to Walter Reed. That was 2003. I was in and out of various military hospitals until 2008, and things weren't improving much. By then, I had developed a dependency on opioids. It was a rough time for Miranda, something needed to be done. I'd had a hundred military doctors up until then, so in desperation, they handed me over to a Dr Levy at a small clinic in New Jersey. I was to stay there in rehab under his supervision for three months. Since then, I've researched this guy on the net, and before that, he was with the CIA, but I reckon he still is. During those three months, I believe I was experimented on because not long after I was released, I began hearing voices."

"Okay, let's leave Dr Levy for now. Tell me about the voices."

While Miranda and Kendy served us coffee and donuts, Dan continued, "For the first couple of years, I thought they were a result of the opioids, you know, the voices seemed like my own thoughts out loud in my head. But in 2013, it started to get weird. The voices started telling me to do things, and it was like they were seeing through my eyes because they'd comment on things."

"Things like what?" I asked.

"Well, at first, it was simple stuff, like they made me masturbate in front of a mirror so they could watch."

"You said 'they'?"

"Yeah, there's a woman and a man."

"Always the same woman and man, right up until now?"

"No, only them when I'm at home. If we go somewhere, they change. It's like going from one 5G network tower to the next, and there's a different operator."

Miranda spoke up, "He explains it like that because he was in digital comms in the forces."

"Right, I get it," Kendy said. "So, you think the military has implanted a chip in you that receives Wi-Fi broadcasts, peer to peer?"

"Yes, and as the coverage has changed over the years, going from 2G now up to 5G, so too has their ability, and the broadcast footprint has widened."

"Like, can you hear them now?" Kendy asked, with a hint of reservation.

"No, but you can be sure they're listening," Dan said.

Kendy and I were finding that a little unnerving.

"So, hey, you're like a mobile bug?" Kendy said.

Miranda added, "No different than a 5G mobile phone; they can already monitor you if they like by turning it on without you knowing it."

"Whoa, that's freaky," Kendy reacted. "I'm like turning mine off."

"It won't matter," Dan said. "They can still listen while it's off."

The look of astonishment on Kendy's face was priceless.

"Have they ever identified themselves to you?" I asked.

"Yes, sure, but only ever the two at home, Andras and Nyx."

I nodded at Kendy, and she immediately began Googling the names on her laptop.

"So when did they first offer up their names?" I inquired.

Dan and Miranda exchanged a glance, and she answered, "It was just after COVID struck in 2020."

"So was that when 5G was introduced?" I questioned.

Kendy looked up, "No, unless it was a trial or military, 5G only officially rolled out here in September 2023, but not everywhere ... it did in Brooklyn and here in Manhattan."

"No, no, I don't think it was that. It was only a couple of days after you got your COVID jab, remember, darling? You blamed it at first," Miranda prompted.

"Yes, I did," Dan recalled, "you know, all those conspiracy theories about the jab carrying a microscopic switch and all."

"Maybe it does," Kendy piped up. "How about this: Andras is the demon of discord, you know, like he stirs up trouble and all, and Nyx is the female demon of night."

"Come to think of it, I only hear from her at night," Dan said.

"Well, she's the one who would have ordered you to do what you did in front of the mirror and all, that's her form," Kendy reported.

"Okay, that might be ... So, have you searched your body for a chip, with a CT scan or something?" I asked.

"Oh yeah, I've had so many X-Rays and scans I probably glow in the dark ... but nothing."

"But were all those scans, etcetera, done by the military?"

"Yes, under veterans' affairs, of course; otherwise, it would have cost a fortune."

"Our only income comes from a VA disability pension," Miranda explained. "Oh, and a few local jobs I pick up."

"Well, then if the military or the CIA experimented on you and inserted a chip to continue with their experiment, they're not going to expose it in a CT scan, are they?" I proposed.

"I guess not," Dan said.

"What did they say when you told them about the voices?" Kendy asked.

"Good question. They said I was suffering from mild schizophrenia due to the opioids and that it would take my nervous system years to repair."

"What a great red herring that is," Kendy scoffed. "Can you stop the voices like while they're talking?" Kendy asked.

"I used to be able to, using this." He handed Kendy a small handheld device about the size of an iPhone. "It's essentially a magnetic RF filter, but it hasn't worked since the COVID jab and more so with 5G."

"And then the really weird thing happened that caused us to contact you. Last week, in the middle of the night, I was woken up by a noise," Miranda explained, "for obvious reasons, we sleep in separate rooms ... the noise was coming from the dining room. I crept out, prepared for a house invader, and found Dan standing in the middle of the room, sleepwalking."

"But how?" Kendy asked.

Dan replied, "We don't know. She walked me back to bed. I had no memory of it in the morning and, of course, still couldn't walk."

"We figured the chip had done something to his nervous system while he was asleep, that got him to walk."

I was deep in thought, trying to make sense of it. The burning question for me was, why. "Dan," I asked solemnly, "there must be a reason they implanted you. What do you think they want from you?"

This time he and Miranda exchanged a secretive glance. She nodded her approval, and Dan said, "The same damn thing they all want to know since it happened."

"All?"

"Every damn doctor, shrink, voice in my head, and especially that Dr Levy. He grilled me every chance he got—I reckon he even hypnotised me."

We were on the edge of our seats. "What was it, Dan?" I repeated.

"They wanted to know the events leading up to the landmine explosion ... it's as if they expect I know some deep secret or something. But hey, it's a total blank."

"What was your division?"

"SEAL Team Five. You can Google us; we were involved in loads of covert operations. Worked with your crowd as well, the Aussies."

"And what was the mission you were on?" I probed deeper.

"We were the advance force into Baghdad, looking for the hiding place of Saddam Hussein."

"And where was the mine?"

"At the entrance to the Baghdad Museum."

I stood up, something had triggered a revelation. I kept it to myself and said, "Okay, that's enough for today. Leave it with us; we'll do some research and then come back to you."

Miranda stood. "About your fee, Mr Stone."

"What fee? Kendy will call you to set up another meeting real soon, maybe at your place—that way I can call in on Book."

Dan held out his hand to shake. "I want to thank you, Axis ... I've gotta tell you, I've never fought alongside braver guys ... blokes, as you say, than the Aussies."

"He got a gold star, you know," Miranda said proudly.

Kendy gave Miranda a hug and a peck on the cheek for Dan, and then showed them to the elevator.

When she returned, I was at my desk, lost in thought.

"What fee?" she barked. "Are we a charity now? First, it was the Harris case, now..."

"Take it easy; we don't need the money. There are more important things than money."

She calmed down and sat on the edge of my desk. "So, what did we learn from all that?"

"In my dream, the uniforms of the military had the symbol of an eagle carrying a trident in front of a V... I could see it as clear as a bell."

"Wait a minute, you think that's connected to Dan, how?"

"The V is five ... it's the symbol of Navy SEAL Team Five, Dan's unit."

Kendy was gobsmacked.

CHAPTER
SEVENTEEN

There was no doubting I had experienced a most profound enlightening experience when Angel entered God's door. The question hounding me was whether it was indeed God's Door as the manuscript described it, or was it some kind of alien visitation experience. One side effect was feeling more at peace with myself than ever before. They say people who return from a near-death experience continue on with no longer fearing death and a desire to embrace life with far more passion—well, that's kind of how I was feeling. Then, quite suddenly, everything changed, all due to another email from Carmen, this time reporting a discovery made by Dr Jax De Ville after deciphering more of the manuscript.

After reading the email, I put my feet up on the desk and tried to connect the dots. Kendy came in soaking wet and shook like a dog. "Why did it have to pour right when I got out of the taxi?"

"Just lucky, I reckon," I taunted.

"Well, you'll be sorry; your croissant got drowned as well."

"You better resuscitate it because we're going to need strong coffees and a croissant for what I'm about to tell you."

That got her attention, and she hopped to it, putting on the coffee and drying out the croissants in the microwave—another new acquisition.

"Pretty soon we'll have an entire kitchen in here," I moaned.

"Ah, Mr Grumpy is back—at last—since you arrived from God's

Door, you've been like a Hari Krishna or something."

I chuckled inwardly, knowing that was exactly what I'd been contemplating. She served up the coffee and croissants.

"So, like tell me then," she said, all ears.

"I got another email from Carmen this morning. It was way different than the last; this was about the palaeographer..."

"Jax De Ville."

"Yep, apparently she had deciphered a large chunk of the manuscript text from where I left off and managed to determine the second item of the sacred three."

"Far out! What is it?"

"The Eridu Genesis tablet."

"Ah, genesis, you said the guy that got killed in Angel's vision said that word... genesis."

"That's right," I was reminded.

"So what's this tablet, and where is it?"

"That's where you come in."

"Research? But wouldn't Jax De Ville know all about it?"

"Yep, but there's no harm in doing our own sniffing around the subject."

"You still think Dan's voices are connected?"

"In some way, I think so."

The phone rang and Kendy got it. She called me from her office. "It Miranda, do you want to take it?"

"Kay," I told her picking up the extension. After a short discussion I hung up and went in to discuss the call with Kendy.

"So, Dan's demon voices, Andras and Nyx, have warned him to stop talking to us otherwise there will be dire circumstances. They even named both of us. I don't get it. Do you think Dan is delusional?"

"I think we to prove that he isn't before we can like progress."

I was pacing the floor, "Hmm, yes, I agree. How about we set a trap for our demons."

"How, they're probably just Ai?"

"I agree but there's someone behind it, Ai can threaten but can't really act, so…"

Kendy was up joining me pacing about. She suddenly stopped with a lightbulb moment. "Got it, how about we like set a rendezvous with Dan and Miranda, but it's a trap for the voice people."

"Exactly, I said you'd make a good PI. That way we'll be able to establish two things, one, if they can monitor Dan's conversations and two if they're real …. If that's the case then they'll turn up to the rendezvous. So to make sure we'll need to make a specific time and place and, a damn good reason to attract them."

"How about the question Dan said they've always been asking?"

"Yes, the truth about what actually happened that day. Let's say Dan's had a dream and written it all down then put it on a flash-drive for us to read and that he'll give it to us at the rendezvous."

"Good call," Kendy said.

The phone rang, and Kendy picked it up. She called me from her office. "It's Miranda, do you want to take it?"

"Okay," I replied, picking up the extension. After a brief discussion, I hung up and went to talk to Kendy.

"So, Dan's demonic voices, Andras and Nyx, have warned him to stop talking to us, or there will be dire consequences. They even mentioned both of us. I don't understand. Do you think Dan is delusional?"

"I think we need to prove that he isn't before we can like make any progress."

I paced the floor, deep in thought. "Hmm, yes, I agree. How about we set a trap for our demon friends?"

"How? They're probably just AI, right?"

"I agree, but there's someone behind it. AI can make threats but can't really take action, so…"

Kendy joined me in pacing the floor and suddenly she stopped with a lightbulb moment. "Got it! How about we set up a rendezvous with Dan and Miranda, but it's a trap for the demons?"

"Exactly! I said you'd make a good PI. That way, we'll be able to establish two things: first, if they can monitor Dan's conversations, and second, if they're real ... If that's the case, then they'll show up at the rendezvous. To ensure that, we'll need to set a specific time and place and come up with a compelling reason to attract them."

"How about the question Dan mentioned they've always been asking?"

"Yes, the truth about what actually happened that day. Let's say Dan's had a dream, wrote it all down, and then put it on a flash drive for us to read, which he'll give us at the rendezvous."

"Good call," Kendy agreed.

It was agreed. We considered the possibility that Miranda's phone was bugged, so I emailed Booker, asking him to print out the instructions and discreetly pass them to Miranda. The message instructed Miranda to inform Dan about the meeting that night, ensuring that Andras and Nyx would eavesdrop on the details of the rendezvous and its purpose, which was to discuss 'the dream' and the exchange of the flash drive. Most importantly, she was not to mention anything beyond that for the entire evening.

The meeting was scheduled for 11 AM at the Starbucks on Canal Street. We had used this location before, and it was perfectly suited for our deception.

~ ~ ~

Just as we were heading out the door of the office for Starbucks, the phone rang. Kendy went back in to get it while I proceeded to the lobby. I had heard the door to Linus' apartment open and wanted to say hello.

"G'Day Linus, what's the news?"

"Has Booker called you yet?"

"No, someone called as we were leaving; Kendy's getting it."

"That'd be him. I only just finished talking to him. He doesn't half go on. Damned if I knew what he was talking about ... something about a Charlie Chan and the manuscript. I told him I haven't seen the movie, but he never shut up about it."

Kendy was coming down the stairs, "Hi Linus. Just spoke to

Booker, he said he spoke to you."

"Did he ask you about the Charlie Chan movie?"

Kendy joined us and gave me a raised eyebrow glance. She humoured Linus, "Yeah, I've seen it, worth a watch."

"Don't know why he gets so wound up about stuff like that these days ... Too much time on his hands and getting old."

He hobbled off back to his apartment, "Bye for now kids. Take care."

We both chuckled and then left the building. It was icy outside, I pulled my collar up, and Kendy pulled on the hood of her hoodie to fight the wind during our brisk ten-minute walk to Starbucks.

With every word turning to steam, I asked Kendy, "So, the movie Charlie Chan and the Manuscript?"

"Miranda knocked on Booker's door first thing this morning and gave him a message for us that the demons know about Charlie Chan and the manuscript."

"Right, so now we have the link ... it's all connected."

"How bizarre. So, why tell Dan that?"

"It was a warning. Whoever they are, they're going after the manuscript. We need to warn Charlie; I'll email him when we get back from Bucks."

~ ~ ~

We entered Starbucks and found Dan and Miranda seated at a table. Only a few patrons were in the place, with loads of vacated tables. I quickly scanned the place for likely suspects but found no-one suspicious. We sat down. I put my finger to my lips to stop either of them from talking. Kendy produced a stack of cards we had made up and flashed the first one. It read, 'Only talk about what to order, no mention of a flash-drive or voices.'

"It's so cold today; I can't wait for a hot latte. Is that what you want, Dan?" Miranda asked.

"Yeah, and one of those egg bites," Dan said enthusiastically.

"Hey, that sounds good. I think I'll copy that." I handed my card to Kendy, and she went to order.

A man in a business suit carrying a newspaper under his arm came in, looked around, then sat at a nearby table for two. He had the Firm written all over him. Dan gave me a look that supported my suspicion. Kendy had given me the deck of cards, I flipped through them and then showed one to Dan.

He dug into his pocket, produced a flash-drive, and handed it to me in silence. I slipped it into my inside coat pocket, making sure the newspaper guy had caught the act. Kendy returned with the coffees and food.

We'd finished our orders in about fifteen minutes. I stood and slyly showed another card to Miranda, then Dan. It read, 'Say goodbye like you'll never see us again and thank us, but you won't be needing our services.'

They complied, and we all made it look genuine. I was betting on the guy with the newspaper, who hadn't ordered, being a tail.

We left, headed for the office.

As we neared the Regis Building, I caught a glimpse in a shop window of my friend from Starbucks tailing us. He was doing a fair job of trying to look inconspicuous. I wondered if he was Andras?

I told Kendy, "You keep going home; I'll take it from here."

She put her head down and walked off into the stiff wind. I entered the building, figuring Andras would be after the flash drive, knowing I had it, and I'd be the target. I wanted Kendy to be clear. I ran up the four flights of stairs, went to the office door, opened it, stepped into the shadows on the landing, leaving the door slightly ajar, and waited.

Only a few minutes later, a shadow stretched across the floor, and Andras, in stealth mode, crept up to the office door. I stepped out of the shadows and pushed my gun into his back. His hands rose immediately.

"Go inside, keeping them up … move!"

He complied.

"Stop," I ordered. "Sit on your hands on the couch … now!"

He did as I instructed. I figured he was in his early thirties; short hair, sharp features ... he certainly fit the profile.

"You with the Firm?"

"No, sir, DIA."

"So why has defence put a tail on me?"

"I can't answer that, sir ... It was my orders."

"I'll put it more clearly for you then, what do you want?"

"The flash drive, sir."

I kept my piece handy and sat on the edge of my desk.

"Okay, I'll make a deal with you. You tell me what I want to know, and I'll give you the flash drive."

"That would depend on whether I can answer your question, wouldn't it?"

"Yes, well, try this: why has Danny Spence been microchipped?"

"For his own protection."

"So you don't deny it."

"No, sir, he signed off on it when he joined up. Nothing illegal."

"That's questionable. What is it you want from him?"

"Only what's on the flash drive."

"His recollection leading up to the landmine explosion."

"Yes, sir."

"Why?"

"I can't answer that, but if you know what's on the flash drive, then you already have an idea."

He had me there. I took the flash drive out of my pocket and held it up for him to see.

"If I don't give it to you—?"

"You will be putting yourself and the Spences in danger."

"From you?"

"No, from others who want the same information."

"Who? Answer me that, and I'll give you the flash drive."

He thought about it long and hard and then said, "The Mukhabarat."

"Here," I said, throwing him the flash drive. It landed on his lap;

he knew better than to release his hands to catch it. "There's nothing on it. The whole thing was a ruse to bring you out into the open and to confirm that Dan Spence wasn't delusional. Go back to your superiors and tell them Dan still can't recall anything. Tell them I will be having the chip removed from him, and if there's any more heat from your people, I'll go public—this guy is a war veteran with a gold star. Do I make myself clear?"

"Yes, sir."

"Are you carrying a weapon?"

"No, sir."

"Okay, release your hands and show me your ID. Slowly."

He put the flash drive in his pocket and then pulled his wallet from his inside coat pocket and flipped it open. I pulled out my phone, went over to him, and took a photo of his ID. "Okay, Paul Sweeney, you can go. Call me if you need more information." I waved my gun at the door. He got up and left.

I immediately emailed Charlie the warning that someone was coming after the manuscript, and it would be up to him to protect it. I also recommended he do a background check on Jax De Ville.

CHAPTER
EIGHTEEN

The Terrible Tango played, and it was Kendy checking on me. I told her I was fine and asked her to set up a meeting with Dan and Miranda here at the office for 10 AM in the morning.

~ ~ ~

I arrived with a box of donuts. Kendy had the coffee brewing.

"I've spent quite some time researching the Eridu Genesis Tablet, and wow, it's amazing," she said, handing me a mug of coffee. "Oh, and by the way, the Spences will be here at 10."

"Okay," I said, sitting behind my desk. "Fill me in on the Eridu Tablet."

Kendy pulled up a chair, eager to share her newly found knowledge. After half an hour and a coffee refill, I was up to speed on the clay tablet that had been unearthed in Nippur in the 19th Century. The single tablet has since been dated at over five thousand years old, and it contains the creation myth in the Sumerian language, although the first part of the story was missing. There was enough of it to get the gist of the story.

"So, there were attempts at translation over the years, but it was eventually translated in 1981 by Harvard Professor Thorkild Jacobson ... but there's a totally different spin on it by Zacharia

Sitchin in his series of novels, the Earth Chronicles," Kendy said.

"We won't go into that now; it seems I've got some homework to do," I admitted with a sigh. "But what do you think are the salient points relating to our situation?"

Kendy opened a notepad and read out her observations, "Well, the first part was always missing but like not so important; the main chunk is now on display at the British Museum, item number K.3375. But in 1987, another piece of it was found at Kouyunjik, that's like the same place in Northern Iraq where the British Museum piece was found in the 19th Century, and it was kept at the Baghdad Museum but went missing during the Iraq War in 2003. I thought it might be relevant, seeing as Dan was there ... like he mentioned the Baghdad Museum and all."

That piqued my interest. "You're right ... the mine exploded outside the museum, he said."

"But hey, I was wondering, if it was like a landmine, why didn't he lose his leg or something?"

"That's a good question, Kendy."

She looked at the clock on the wall and was surprised, "Oh wow, the Spences will be here any minute."

"Okay, put on some more coffee, they'll probably need warming up."

I checked my email and there was a reply from Charlie. He wanted more details on who might be coming to steal, the manuscript. He said Mukhabarat was too broad a term, as every Middle Eastern country has a secret service referred to as the Mukhabarat. It simply means secret service, but generally refers to the General Intelligence Directorate of Iraq, though it was dissolved in 2003 and is now called the Iraqi National Intelligence Service (INIS). He added that Carmen had run a check on De Ville, and she'd come up clean. I replied, telling him to 'watch this space,' intending to find out the identity of the potential threat, but I mentioned I had a run-in with the Firm; he'd know my meaning.

Just as I hit send, there was a knock at the door. Kendy showed in Miranda and Dan. Once we were settled with coffee and donuts, I filled him in on my discussion with Agent Paul Sweeney of the DIA and the resolution. They were pleased, not only with the resolution but with the fact that the voices had finally been confirmed.

"So I'm not nuts then," Dan said sarcastically.

"Not as far as we can tell," I joked.

Quite emotional, Miranda said, "You don't know what it means to us to finally be vindicated."

"At least now we can get the chip removed," I proposed. "VA will arrange that."

"Not yet," Dan appealed. "Damn if that thing could get me to walk that once, then hell, maybe it could fix me permanently."

"I wanted to ask you, Dan," Kendy said, "did you sustain any other injuries from the explosion? Like, how near to it were you?"

"You did say you were walking into the Baghdad Museum," I added.

"Well now, like I've said, I don't remember much ... but I'll tell you, what I've never told them, you know all them asking me ... I wasn't walking into the Museum, we was walking out of the place."

"I see ... so you and how many others?"

"There were three of us; we were the first in ... the rest of our team was tied down across town ... it was night. We'd made it across Shuhada Bridge; it had taken plenty of hits but was still standing, just ... not far was the Al-Zawraa Park, there were snipers on the other side of it ... we got through and crossed Zaytoun Street under fire. The objective was to meet up with the rest of our unit closing in on the Harthiya Intelligence Center, on the other side of the Baghdad Museum. One of our guys reckoned there was loot to be had in the museum, so we made a diversion to grab what we could. Once we got into the street, it was easy going in the dark. We reached the museum without any trouble and then broke in through a side door. I remember being inside; our flashlights were lighting up all these crazy artefacts on display. We grabbed what we could, packed it away, and then busted out through the front door. I've obviously had to keep that a secret all this time."

"Wasn't there an alarm or something?" I asked.

"No, the place had taken a couple of big hits from the air, and all power to the city was cut."

"Go on?" I prompted.

"This part I remember like it was yesterday because there were these weird storm clouds with strange lightning above us, then the light, a blinding light like a laser beam came out of nowhere and hit the guy who wanted to rob the museum ... like it was the storm's vengeance ... the last thing I can remember was looking up for the source of the light ... damn thing looked like it was coming from outer space. Next thing I woke up in the hospital unable to walk, the skin on my face and forearms blistered like from radiation."

The whole story was sounding very familiar to me.

"What was the diagnosis?" I asked.

"Massive nerve damage..."

"Peroneal paralysis, I was told," Miranda said.

Kendy asked, "What happened to the other two guys?"

"They said the guy in the beam was like petrified, turned to stone ... and the other guy ... I don't know; they flew him home, I heard."

"And the loot?" I asked.

"Got no idea," Dan declared.

"What was the other guy's name, the one flown home?"

"Grant McCloud ... we were friends, but I never heard from him again."

"Where was he from?"

"Arizona, if I remember rightly, Apache Junction I think, near Phoenix."

I asked Dan and Miranda if they'd like us to contact Veteran's Affairs to arrange for them to look into how the chip could have made Dan sleepwalk. They agreed, and then went on their way.

Kendy and I discussed what we'd learned.

"That was almost a word-for-word description of the laser beam at Lindos Resort, right down to the same way Vinny Vitale was virtually vitrified by it."

Kendy was amazed. "I know, I know, like unbelievable, even down to the blistered skin. But none of you guys suffered nerve damage."

"No, but maybe that was caused by something else, perhaps he fell over and was knocked out, you know blinded by the light ... he doesn't remember anything after looking up at it. I wonder what they'd stolen from the museum?"

"I think that's obvious," Kendy said with a big smirk.

"What?"

"The chunk of the Eridu Tablet that was on display that went missing in 2003."

"No way..." I exclaimed in astonishment. "That's what this had all been about ... the second object of the sacred three."

"Yes, the tablet probably like needs to be intact."

"You know, I reckon you're right on the money, Kendy."

This case was far from over, we needed to track down the missing piece of the Eridu Tablet last known to be with Grant McCloud, twenty years ago, possibly in Arizona. Charlie needed to safeguard the manuscript from being hijacked, and now it was obvious it was up to us to secure the next item in the sacred three. Now that's quite enough for any bloke to have on his plate don't you reckon?

Don't miss the continuing adventure
in Book Six:

"The Sacred Three"

www.ingramcontent.com/pod-product-compliance
Lightning Source LLC
Chambersburg PA
CBHW020528120726
47904CB00003B/1002